THE LITTLE HAMMER

John Kelly

Jonathan Cape
London

Published by Jonathan Cape 2000

2 4 6 8 10 9 7 5 3 1

Copyright © John Kelly 2000

John Kelly has asserted his right under the Copyright, Designs
and Patents Act 1988 to be identified as the author of this work

First published in Great Britain in 2000 by
Jonathan Cape
Random House, 20 Vauxhall Bridge Road,
London SW1V 2SA

Random House Australia (Pty) Limited
20 Alfred Street, Milsons Point, Sydney,
New South Wales 2061, Australia

Random House New Zealand Limited
18 Poland Road, Glenfield,
Auckland 10, New Zealand

Random House South Africa (Pty) Limited
Endulini, 5A Jubilee Road, Parktown 2193, South Africa

The Random House Group Limited Reg. No. 954009
www.randomhouse.co.uk

A CIP catalogue record for this book
is available from the British Library

ISBN 0 224 06044 9

Papers used by Random House UK Limited are natural,
recyclable products made from wood grown in sustainable forests.
The manufacturing processes conform to the environmental
regulations of the country of origin

Typeset by Palimpsest Book Production Limited,
Polmont, Stirlingshire
Printed and bound in Great Britain by
Biddles Ltd, Guildford and King's Lynn

FOR CATHERINE

'Someday darlin', I'm going down that 'lantic side.
Someday darlin', I'm going down that 'lantic side.
With my hammer in my hand,
Gonna catch that evil wave and ride.'

Atlantic Ocean Blues (Trad.)

CONTENTS

IF I HAD A HAMMER

Would you believe me if I told you that I was only nine years of age when I killed him? Would you believe me if I told you that I killed him stone dead and that the granny was mortified – that she nearly woke the whole street roaring –

Jesus, Mary and Joseph! We'll all be lifted!

Would you believe me if I told you that a mackerel-nibbled corpse was hauled back on to the bruising Donegal rocks and that a rum boatload of fishermen took the Holy Name, turned their faces away and ran screaming for the Guards?

Would you believe me if I told you that I watched the creamy old ambulance sweeping past the Holy Infant of Prague on my windowsill and that I knew that my victim was flat out inside – all purple and yellow and stiff as a board? Would you believe me if I said that it was the granny herself who took the hold of everything?

There's no proof! she announced on the minute, no evidence! Not one iota! And you can't be summonsed without evidence!

And she was right – there was no evidence at all and so it appears that a certain chilling family silence ensured that I remained both at liberty and

at myself. This solemn and onerous sealing of the lips had been firmly guaranteed (as was the custom) by a sudden get-together in a local hotel – a depressing gather-up, predictably well attended by the aunts, the uncles and the hateful buckteeth cousins – the whole shower presided over by the grandmother herself –

There might be a lot of oul talk round the town, she said calmly, a load of oul nonsense about the wee fella there. But I don't want to hear another word about it. Not one word or we'll all end up in the Barracks! Do yous hear me? We'll all end up in the Barracks!

Of course nobody except me had any idea what she was talking about but, even so, she made everyone swear a terrible oath 'on your granny's grave' and this, despite its inherent lack of logic, was spoken with great gravitas by all. For added security every-one crossed their hearts and hoped to die and I immediately felt more secure and was noticeably happier in myself.

That should perhaps have been the end of it but then the paranoia set in. I began to fear that perhaps such pledges of silence might not apply to she who administers it and that, in no time at all, it would be the grandmother herself who would be spilling the hills of beans all over the country. I grew suddenly afraid that she might in fact be mad to talk about it, that she would love nothing more than to spread it around and that she would relish every last detail of the whole horrific episode and make it her very own.

And so I lived for a period in empty-stomached terror that it might become a story held exclusively by her only to be passed on in accordance with the oral tradition every bleak wet Christmas in the flickering TV glow – the whole brutal saga annually embellished and trumpeted into the little pink ears of the new grandchildren born to the hateful buck-teeth cousins, none of whom could be trusted in a fit –

Hit him full whack with a pickaxe no less! she would tell them. Killed him stone dead! Dead as a do-er nail! Went over like a sack o' spuds!

And best of it all, the grandmother only had my word for it. She hadn't been within an ass's roar of the place. At the time of the said offence, she was on the two knees gazing at a gable wall in Knock in the County of Mayo – channelling rosary beads between finger and thumb and concentrating hard on the bad back. She had a terrible bad back and many's the time I took her to the Well of the Holy Women to get the cure.

I'll tell you this for nothing – it certainly was no pickaxe – not a pickaxe pickaxe – not one of those Council flagbusters a sunburnt man in a vest might swing above his head on a sweltering day. This item was a much smaller and more refined instrument – a kind of mini pickaxe used exclusively for tapping lightly and picking delicately at fragile layers of rock. It was, to be precise, a geological hammer and it belonged to the man himself – the one who got clocked.

3

The deceased was by vocation a palaeontologist – a devotee of extinct beings – a collector of fossils. And he looked the part too in the red windcheater, the green waterproof trousers and the black woollen cap. Other than that, all he had was the grey canvas bag with the cartoon dinosaur patch sewed on to it and the famous little pickaxe. I don't know the man's name.

We met when I was hoking about in the rocks – just the sort of thing a virtual only child does to put in the day. Back then I would have spent hours hoking and poking in rockpools – picking at anemones and hermit crabs and catching plasticky, rubbery shrimps with a green gauze net on a bamboo pole – sweeping hopefully for crabs and baby fish the colour of sand. Driven by the hidden treasure of it, I risked fingers and thumbs to drag up mussels and cockles and whelks and winkles – sometimes a sea mouse or a spiny urchin. If I was quick enough, a limpet caught on the hop.

But buggerlugs the palaeontologist wasn't hoking for living things. He was after the millions of fossils which lay everywhere in the limestone. They were everywhere – what I thought were little broken backbones of fish – vertebrae, slipped discs, miniature tree-trunks in a miniature fallen forest. I knew places where you could see whole shells – only they were not real shells – they were rocks. Ancient sea animals turned to stone, silvery and perfect, like they'd just gawked at the Gorgon. Ammonites. Lower Jurassic. It said in a book that it was to do with Saint Hilda

4

and petrified headless serpents – but that was only baloney.

When I noticed head-the-ball tapping away with his geological hammer I got curious and bold and began to orbit ever closer. He chipped and tapped away for hours and carefully wrapped little bits of Roguey Rock in cotton wool and put them in his bag. I thought it was a very odd way of passing the time when the pools were boiling with big monster crabs with big nippers that would cut the toes off you. It was a puzzle.

What are you doing, mister? I asked eventually.

He smiled and said that he was collecting fossils and asked me did I know what fossils were. I said I did surely and told him that there were millions of them. He held up a fossil shell and told me that it was a brachiopod.

What are you collecting them for, I asked.

I'm a palaeontologist.

A what?

A palaeontologist. I collect fossils.

Do you sell them? I asked.

No I don't sell them, he replied patiently, I study them.

I wondered did he get much homework and he indicated that I could come over and have a closer look. That is exactly the circumstance in which I met the palaeontologist and how, more to the point, I ended up with the pickaxe [*sic*] in my hand. Pass no remarks on what you might have heard – especially from the granny. She wasn't there and, anyway, she might have been wandering.

Our little secret, she said over and over again, you just say nothin', son, or the whole lot of us will end up in Castlereagh!

BEAUTIFUL BUNDORAN

To carry a terrible secret for twenty-one years of a thirty-year-old life is an awful and destructive thing. To talk about it now will be, for me, as good as a tonic – like a weekend on Lough Derg or a good boke. Forget all oaths on grannies' graves. Forget the summons and the Barracks. Talk! Tell the story! It may explain much of the carry-on and caper and so, first we take Bundoran.

All of the grannies and all of the mothers have taken the bus to Bundoran. In their cardigans and blowy skirts they have skipped over the marram and laughed that distant, echoey, beachy laughter – free to flirt with all of the grandfathers and all of the fathers in their white shirts and galluses and hardly the price of a silent cone between them. Everywhere, bare feet and white shins. A wind blowing in from Manhattan, the stink of mulching seaweed and a sky and sea of pure, endless distance.

From all over Fermanagh and Tyrone, trainloads, generations, whole connections and tribes have landed in Bundoran to paddle or swim, to sit on walls and kick their ankles. All of the headscarfed grannies and all of the headscarfed mothers on the arms of all of the silent grandfathers and all of the silent fathers –

shivering into each other with the very first signs of a kiss. Roguey Rock. The West End. The Nuns' Pool. I was part of all that. Part of the holiday. Part of the pilgrimage.

The Triumph Herald came down the hill and, over the rooftops, I saw the new colour of the sea – the sheer space of it and frightening wildness of it. The money-making streets were teeming and everyone was in a brand-new mode – shorts, open shirts, no shirts, big fat women with big fat legs, varicose veins, children hung with buckets, rings and towels and the odd Donegal dog with a bit of a want searching in vain for a sheep.

Arrival here was as exotic to me as arrival in an Eastern bazaar or a spicy medieval market place of jugglers, snake-charmers and dancing bears. My sparrow heart pounded and my father, the slayer of the moo-moos said, game ball!

Sliding from the leathery heat of the car, the breeze and the brightness feathered around my bare legs and I breathed a fierce impatience for sand, the thump of music from the hobby-horses and the deadly scream-ing swingboats. Rugs and towels were gathered and the Cherokee women asked us for coppers. Always the Cherokee women wrapped in red blankets – sad-faced with jet-black Cherokee hair and a big baby's bald head hanging out like a heavy round breast. Gypsies they were called, itinerants, tinkers – made pots and pans and lived in caravans. I thought of wigwams, tomahawks and bareback mustangs.

God bless yis, the Cherokee women would say.

The seagulls squealed above me and my heart thundered like the rollers themselves. Grown-ups were different. They were slower, calmer, more sensible –

Now, go to the toilet before you go down to the beach!

And I would go off with my father to the greening whitewashed toilets – Fir meant men and Mná meant women. They were open to the sky and this was weird too – my gutties on the concrete, peeing against the rough whitewash in a silent line of boozy men spitting long, drooly spits.

And then the town slowly transformed into beach. The hot tarmac of the roads began to get sandy as drifts of alien gold were blown up on to the streets. The feel of it under my feet was strange and wrong and everything was on its head. The sounds around me began to dampen into a strange dreamy squealing and I inhaled the fading trebly wash from the funfair and the sweet sickly smell of hairy candyfloss got in my nose. And then down the slope and on to the beach, I ran hard and fearless – like a dog out of a trap –

Be careful now! You'll break your neck!

Off with the sandals –

Watch there's no glass there!

Off with the shirt –

Now watch you don't get burnt!

And then the struggle with the towel and the trunks as I got the shorts and the underpants off and got the swimming trunks on without anybody seeing anything – especially ladies. It was something to do with a thing called modesty and whenever they said that the uncle was a great singer but was very modest about it, I knew that meant that he never took his knickers off in front of ladies when he was singing.

I couldn't see why anybody would want to look at your lad anyway. Maybe it was because ladies didn't have lads. Skunk Sheridan always called his lad his tool. What's the rule? he would say, mind your tool.

And so I just minded my tool and ran like the hammers – elbows and knees slicing in all directions and sprinting headlong at the Atlantic Ocean. Geronimo! Last one in's a rotten egg!

As the first freezing shock hit my toes I would pull up and make a high-pitched skidding noise with the back of my throat. This was far enough. This was the deep, dark sea full of currents and undercurrents and cross-currents. Heaving with tides and shifting sands and quick sands and tangling weeds. Boiling with jellyfish and sharks and stingrays and the eight-legged giant octopus. Full to the lip with actual helpless death. And so I would paddle there in silence like a great white innocent heron, picking at shells – dry as a bone from the knees up.

As for the actual dispatch of our man the fossil collector – it was like this. Simple enough. We were at the far end of Roguey – next parish Manhattan. He was on his hunkers examining something and I was holding the geological hammer, enjoying the grain of it, the weight of it, the threat of it. I gently tested it a few times against the palm of my hand and found it a hugely satisfying instrument. The initials P. M. were engraved in the handle and wouldn't it be funny, I thought, if he was the Prime Minister?

I gazed at the back of his head until my eyes lost focus and blurred cross-eyed and all his talk about the limestone and the fossils began to fade away. Soon I could hear only my own blood pumping in my own ears. Thu-dump! Thu-dump! Thu-dump! Thu-dump! Next thing I cracked him full whack on the back of the head. Very matter-of-fact.

Would you believe me if I told you that he didn't make a sound apart from a bit of a groan and that he simply lurched forward and banged the forehead against the rock? Would you believe me if I said that I just stood back as he made a weak effort to get up but that the legs had already gone from under him? That he staggered and tumbled sideways over the ledge and fell quietly into the green frothy waves. Would you believe me if I told you that that was end of him and that I quietly buggered off? Jakers, I whispered to myself, the granny will have my life.

LEVIATHAN

Before we go any further, let me now take a bucklep out of the foregoing and deal with present-day realities. I am no longer nine years old – I am thirty years old and, as the grandmother would say, I'm like the Wreck of the Hesperus.

I am at liberty and at large and I am an artist no less – these days preferring the sable brush to the geological hammer. I've been mixing paint since cockcrow and doing it, I must confess, without much sense of purpose. Nothing's getting done and the place – my studio – my space – looks like a bomb hit it.

In fact, a bomb did hit it once. Strange when you think about it now but it was one of those home-made mortars – a DIY job meant for the Barracks. I was certain sure I was going to be lifted when the soldiers arrived – bomb disposal with Bugs Bunny on the truck. They were here half the day, plodding around in spacesuits and talking to themselves about their wives and Bolton Wanderers. Eventually they left without a word and, according to a moustachioed peeler with pimples on his neck, they had successfully defused it – the device as he called it.

Meat and drink to boys like that, he said.

But for all I know the damn thing is still up there – live and ticking and rolling about on the slates. Was it Bugs Bunny or was it Daffy Duck? I forget now. Maybe it was Tweetie Pie? That was the granny's favourite. She used to roar laughing at him saying, I tought I taw a puddytat! –

And sure them's only drawin's, she would say, isn't that what that is? Only drawin's and them movin' about the place and singing and dancing and runnin' after other. Isn't it wonderful what they can do?

I haven't painted anything much for about six months. The last thing I did was a huge canvas the width of this room. It was a crazy-looking coot on a kind of viridian, bluey background. A big massive coot! It should have been black with a white beak – but mine was bright, bright, bright yellow with a red beak. It looked great. God knows why I painted it yellow but I beat it on with a big brush and it worked so well you could have put your two hands under its beating breast and carried it back all heart-thumping to the rushes. I was well pleased with it. It was bought by some kind of suit from the BBC who wanted something expensive and yellow for his office. Fair enough.

I have always loved the solid shapes of the coot and the waterhen. Wasn't I was reared with them? Just like Romulus and Remus growling around the Tiber with their lupine mother, I was brought up yolky, muddy and wet with the fussy waterfowl of the Erne. I know and love their every move – arching up off the lough or plashing across the water into low, determined flight. A week later I painted a purple one but it wasn't worth a damn. Painted over it. A complete hames.

Ornithological interlude:

The coot or *Fulica atra* as smart men call it, comes from the family Rallidae – the rails – like *Rallus aquaticus* (the water rail), *Crex crex* (the landrail or corncrake) and the *Gallinula chloropus* (the waterhen). Rather like a big waterhen with a white beak, the coot possesses grotesque, unlikely feet with big lobed toes for the miraculous walking on the water. It makes very sharp noises (which I could mimic for you at the drop of a hat) but at other times its call is as mellow as a rolling bream on a calm April evening. When we were cubs we called them baldies and their sonic echo was as soothing to me as the curlew of the curlew, the drum of the snipe or the jangle of the ice-cream van. If we saw a bald man we would say –

Lookit! that baldy bastard's as bald as a coot!

It's a long time now since I was a cub and those idyllic murderous days in Bundoran and the glarry loughshore – a quare long time. These days I'm tall, thin, single, paranoid and white-knuckled – an El Greco stretch of gaunt aspect given to wondering about what exactly is going on the half the time. My clothes, like myself, are ill-fitting – trousers at half-mast, jacket like a bag and shirt all creased. The hair is still reasonably long – but standing on me.

The best thing about me is that I'm easy pleased. I remember once being flat out on a rug in the backyard watching the late swifts harpooning themselves about in a clear sky and it suddenly and briefly coming to me that I was completely content. It was so pure a moment – transcendental and no bullshit and I realised I was happy as the day actually was long – honest to God prepared at that very moment to have been assumed into heaven – closer to the screeching swifts, the jet trails and the warm setting sun. Such mystical moments, I have come to accept, are like coots' teeth. Especially in the circumstances.

My paintings are somewhere between the wild and the straightforward representational. They are never totally abstract – but having said that, there are times when you couldn't quite put your finger on what the hell they are. The grandmother says that a child could do better and sometimes I think she's right.

There is a certain celebrity that comes with it and I make good money. My paintings, even small shite ones, go for large sums and I am constantly asked to appear on long-winded arts programmes about nothing in particular. I hate all that palaver but those are the pincer jaws of it. What can you do?

Everything about my existence is full of painful contradictions and what makes the curse worse is that I'm fully aware of them. Cases in point. I love the smell of bluebells and wild garlic and yet I live in this scrapyard city. I am reclusive and yet I have to appear in public. I paint coots yellow and I murdered a palaeontologist when I was nine.

All in all, it's neither bowl of cherries nor sweet lorraine.

The studio itself is certainly a tip but the rent is cheap and even when I'm getting nothing done I still hover here. Part discipline but also as a kind of exercise in itself. It's as if I must stay on watch – just in case something happens – which of course is the height of bollocks. I'd be better off out looking at coots and soaking up shapes in the changing light.

To tell you the truth, at times like these, I just mix the paint and gaze at all those gleaming rolls of colour and crush them into rainbows with a butter knife. On days like these it's not that I can't paint – it's more that there is nothing *to* paint. And that's a real snooker.

Eventually I read the old newspapers. I always read old newspapers and there's a great comfort in it because there are no shocks. Everything has already happened and cannot touch me now. To know more than the newspaper makes a man feel omniscient and secure. Like falling asleep with the radio on – dreaming the news – then waking up familiar with all details of morning bulletins. It lifts me out of real time and jolts me from the logic of happenings, out of the curving Universe, chronology, human helplessness and the dread of extreme unction.

And in the paper:

ATTEMPT TO BURY WHALE TODAY

Funny enough – a photograph of a dead fifty-three-foot whale washed ashore at Beautiful Bundoran. As in all such photographs, there are lonely figures standing with their hands in their pockets and looking on as helpless as the whale had been – squeezed out on the rocks like a giant slug of barnacled paint. The people are Lilliputian and Gulliver's great lungs have been crushed by his own weight – dead to all prodding and sad observation. Mr Dick Richards from the Council, who had been appointed to dispose of the whale, said that when a cetacean dies it inflates with gas and can possibly explode.

Rubbing my neck with the palms of my hands, I glanced towards the ceiling and imagined the explosion – the flying slates – the Bangor Blues, the pots of paint, the blue-white guts, the tubes, the Winsor and Newton, the blubber, the Barracks, the canvas, the whale oil and all the ragged bloody bits – the stench of gas – a flaming Zeppelin and all the fiery dirigible smithereens of it in all directions. I've often heard of cows exploding – swelling up like methane balloons and bang! I've never seen it happen but any farmer will tell you.

Here was the conundrum. Donegal County Council was stuck with a carcass. Not much point in towing the corpse out into the waves because it would only get washed back in again with the tide – like our man, the palaeontologist. And so came the clever part of this whole Bundoran episode. Killybegs Seaworld urged Donegal County Council to bury the whale pronto. After a period they would exhume the skeleton and put it on show as part of its cetacean display,

The whale is dead, said Ms Siobhan Martin, spokeswoman for Killybegs Seaworld, by preserving its skeleton and putting it on display, it may give visitors an image of what a real whale looks like.

A good idea! A very good idea! A marvellous idea! An idea which indicates, if nothing else, that even the massive reeking rot of the world's largest body can be lithely skipped in the human mind. I was very moved by the whole thing. A fifty-three-foot whale. A female. A mother. A mammal. I thought of a baby whale, a womb and mother's milk.

And of course nobody is in any hurry to bury her because her magnificent shining body has become a tourist attraction and local publicans are having an off-season pay day – smartarses asking for a whale on the rocks.

For the rest of the day I painted, many times over, a creature I had never seen – my mind informed only by the newspaper photograph and memories of a scarred Gregory Peck chasing the great white whale – Leviathan swallower of Jonah. The huge forms I painted were purples and reds, others were ochre and green – barnacled, lichened and stained like rocks. I would never show them to anyone – so awful was the terror in their pearly eyes – helpless on an old canvas the size of that wall.

One day, I thought to myself, I will go to Bundoran and caress her whitening chalky bones. In the meantime I would remember her now and again like a dead friend or relation – like a razor shell, like my own sunburnt legs or like the Holy Infant of Prague buried twenty years ago, upright and solid in the clabbery sand.

THE HOLY FAMILY

There was a time when I was neither a nine-year-old, a murderer or, for that matter, a painter of weirdy pictures. There had, of course, been a swift and comparatively pure decade prior to that particular July day on Roguey Rock and it was a sweet, blessed and easy time.

My recollection of those innocent days is like a dry boke and throws up very little of consequence – but having said that, what there is of it, is both vivid and significant. And so now, to the best of my ability, a childhood reminiscence – my early days – and an incorrupt tongue.

Is it odd that I well remember being in the cot – a rickety construction with yellow bars and fences? I seem to recall too that there was a strange liquid freedom to be experienced by pushing my cherubic hands, arms and feet through these bars and grills and out into the smoky air. A dangerous liberation right enough.

For company in the cot I had a brown woollen rabbit with no ears and a soft representation of what I believed was a dog as bald as a coot. The dog was called Lugs and the rabbit was called Bugs and they slept on either side of my angelic little curly blond head. Oh, Angel of God, my guardian dear. Some nights I could hardly get to sleep such was the brightness of the light from the baby halo.

I spent some several years in this cot patiently waiting to be sprung. But in the end I had to arrange my own escape by learning to stand, stagger, gate-vault and toss the place. By then I had also acquired some primitive speech and my first word is reported by the grandmother to have been *gyetthahelloutathat!* – a rare compound word often overheard in my district. What I actually said was more along the baby-talk lines of *giddadadilldahelladelataslcatat* and I apparently said it in response to the father pretending to be a crane and attempting to feed me creamed rice with a fork.

O-pen up, that's the cub. O-pen up, here it comes! O-pen up. Ah go on! O-pen up! Will you open up! Open up! Will you open your mouth and ate your dinner ye ungrateful wee skitter!

And so I said *giddadadilldahelladelataslcatat.*

As I developed my powers of observation I began to realise that we were as a family afflicted by the realities of a certain poverty but that in spite of this, we were not at all happy. The father reeked perpetually of the moo-moos and John Player Specials and the mother forever waved ferocious kitchen implements at the grandmother who called her names and talked openly of sailors.

Only the mother would dare to confront the grandmother and whenever this happened the father would be mortified. Mine was a rare and ancient clan and the grandmother reigned over it imperiously. Her empire, her diaspora, her whole blood connection was a rum shower of specimens of various dimensions and altitudes but was not recognised as such by her. To the grandmother, they were for the most part worthy of some kind of vicious love and the tribe in turn prayed God to save her and bless her, followed her every instruction and acted promptly on her every whim.

When not marching about our house simultaneously saying the rosary and giving out yards, she lived alone and nearby in a quasi-church smelling of briquettes and baking bread which sat serenely in the corner of the estate in the corner of the glen. It was a fine pebble-dashed Housing Executive home overtaken by icons and statues of holy men and women who gave her good example in the art of suffering and the offering up of the thing. She drank only cold tea and ate exclusively of a mysterious grey paste called Forola. She was always a good granny even so and she gave me money and boiled sweets out of her overall pockets. If the money fell on the lino she would say there was luck in it.

I was her favourite. One of the relations had once complained that the granny thought 'the sun shone out of my arse' and never gave any money to any of her buckteeth offspring but the granny told her to have a titter of wit and that was the end of it. Even so, it was clear that she couldn't stand some of them and reserved most of her affection and her thrupenny bits for me. After the Bundoran episode we were even closer – bound together by our deadly and shivery secret.

Not a word out of you! Do you hear me talkin' to you? Say nothin'!

I do not propose to examine any further the unpleasant appearances, clothing or habits of the myriad buckteeth cousins and their progenitors, but I think it appropriate at this juncture to relay a tad more detail concerning my immediate family – odd figures who populated that idyllic childhood spent in front of the magic lantern watching *The Banana Splits* and *The Flashing Blade* and, in rare windy interludes, spent putting palaeontologists to death on the wild western seaboard of our sideways doggy-shaped land.

The father worked in the meat factory and had strong wrists. His function in life, as far as my strong suspicions went, was the sudden and allegedly humane dispatch of moo-moos. In his earlier days he had supposedly worked as a professional wrestler, circus strongman, hod carrier, longshoreman, barrel-maker and nightclub bouncer and his name was Big Francie. A small person, he was the grandmother's favourite son.

The mother, rumoured at the time to have been of English extraction, was never talked about. She had worked on a poultry farm somewhere outside the town and had been gainfully employed in chopping the astonished heads off banty hens. I remember nothing much of her presence other than her night-marish bedtime tales of Vesuvian headless chickens steeplechasing around the crimson-splattered yard.

Even with their little heads off, she whispered, they can still run around the place. Cluck! Cluck! Cluck! Now off you go to sleep that's a good boy. Nighty-night.

She disappeared one blowy day when I was about four and reportedly took herself off over to England – across the water. The grandmother at once gave an all-knowing nod and hissed in my ear that she had run away with a sailor. I found it hard to believe, however, that she could ever meet a sailor where we lived – us being so far from the heaving green waves of our rocky romantic shores. A greengrocer perhaps, a coalman, a lollipop man, a postman, a digger-driver, a breadman, a tanned German perhaps with yellow wellies and a cruiser boat – but never a sailor. I was almost certain of that. It was funny all the same. The sailor was Popeye and she was Olive Oyl.

This strange naval allegation always made me uneasy, confused and slightly orphaned. In those days I was unacquainted with the technicalities of human behaviour – the snipe, the great crested grebe and the mallard duck being more within my empirical ambit given the many hours spent wallowing in the glar round Buttermilk Point and beyond. Anything to do with human beings and their activities was always hushed up into hisses and digs in the ribs.

I had an alleged sister too but well dare you mention her either! She had been optimistically christened Attracta but grew up with the pet name of Boot and I remember that I both liked and hated her in roughly equal measure. We would fight all the time and she would scrab the face off me.

At the age of seventeen she was suddenly, *ex-cathedra*, declared a non-person and angrily banished – bell, book and candle – to live with a buckteeth second cousin in the Free State. I was never ever told what she had done. All I knew was that she had fallen in with some student priest from the normally theologically dependable county of Monaghan and had accompanied him to the local picture house. Whenever, in later years, I asked the grandmother what Boot had supposedly done that was so bad, she always said –

Oh Jesus, Mary and Joseph!

Whenever I asked my father about it, he always advised me to ask the grandmother. It was an absurd yet unbreakable loop and nobody ever told me anything about anything. It was like talking to the wall.

I had never had any brothers and I was glad. Everybody else's brothers were wee bastards that squealed on them all the time and whenever crowds of us played together in the reed-beds and potholes, the first hour was always wasted trying to chase them away. They were pukes and pests and tell-tale tits and they always wanted to go to the toilet, jumping up and down and gripping their lads through their trousers. Sometimes I imagined that I had an invisible wee brother but I didn't like him either.

I was therefore *de facto* and quite happily (though not technically) an only child – something which definitely has me the way that I am. Even so, I was never in any particular way groomed for murder. Certainly the tribe could be rough enough in places – indeed one of the buckteeth cousins who was known as Jonty the Goat would rise a row at the drop of a hat. A crabbed wee bugger, the granny called him. Fight with his own shadow.

But by and large we were, at the granny's insistence, a peaceable contingent who avoided sins of a mortal nature and contented ourselves with the venial. It was also the grandmother's priority to avoid drawing the attention of the police and the judiciary to the favourite but murderous grandson – the cub.

THE QUIET MAN

When I think now of the shiny nuns who gazed on me with delight when I made my first confession and communion at the age of seven. They were always tickled pink by the sinless and the pure and up until the age of ten I could have easily passed for that – a little saint no less – especially in the dim darkness of the confession box, its black void echoing sinful whispers above me.

Bless me, Father, for I have sinned. This is my first confession. I told lies. I soaked the mother with the hosepipe. I called the father a flipper and I didn't do what the grandmother told me. For these, and for all my sins, I am very sorry.

And what, child dear, did the grandmother ask you to do?

Go down the town, Father – for the *Fermanagh Herald* and a packet of Forola. I didn't want to go because I had a sore foot from kicking the coal shade.

And why were you kicking the coal shed?

I don't know, Father. I must have taken the headstaggers.

But son, you shouldn't be kicking coal sheds.

It was my own coal shade, Father.

Nevertheless.

Is it a sin to kick the coal shade, Father?

Well, son, what did the coal shed ever do on you?

It was just in the road, Father.

When I came out the hushing Tardis door and knelt with lines of other young sinners I knew that I hadn't been very impressive. I didn't really have anything of note to reveal and I wondered if perhaps I should have made something up. Stealing a bicycle or an Action Man out of Wellworth's? Stabbing the grandmother with the priddie knife? Giving the two fingers to the insurance man?

I knew the rest of the boys had all lied through their jagged teeth. Murdering people and robbing banks and committing adultery with the neighbour's ox. I knew because they all looked so proud of themselves as they emerged one by one from the blackness and pretended to pray hard for the forgiveness they were glad they needed. I just looked at the lines of radiator pipes and wondered where they went – taking with them the sins of the faithful – or at least those of us who could think of any.

And then first communion. The new outfit the grandmother had picked out at the Mart. A navy blazer with shiny buttons, brown short trousers, white ankle socks, black shoes, a lime-green shirt and a ginger-coloured tie with an elastic band around the neck. I looked a sight – a white prayerbook in my hand and a gummy smile that said please give me 10p I'm a lovely wee cub.

The boys sat on one side and the girls tottered into their seats on the other – all dressed like little brides – white handbags, crooked National Health specs and flesh-coloured eyepatches over one eye.

When we filed back from the altar, hands joined and dripping in rosary beads, we knelt and waited for something miraculous as the cardboardy bread dissolved on our tongues. Again I looked around me – rubbernecking at the choir, the pipes of the organ and all the serious expressions on the faces of my fellow gargoyle communicants. The grandmother said she was as proud as punch. Said I was like a wee angel.

So don't for a minute think that I was reared in an environment where it was considered acceptable to clock a fossil collector with his own hammer. In fact, it was the other way entirely – with the grandmother it was all holy Joe and holy medals every time you walked out the door. Holy water flew in all directions and a thousand prayers were urgently whispered to ward off any of the evil that might befall me out in the world of gallivanters, quare cowboys and bad women. That plus her endless deference to the ancient customs and pistrix of the district meant that I was never in what you might call a cold, unprincipled or Godless state. In fact, as alluded to earlier, I was at the time of the Bundoran splash going through quite a spell of religious mania.

Not altogether surprisingly therefore, there has been the odd occasion when a sudden guilty fear bubbled up in my stomach. No surprise really given that the grandmother was forever rambling away like Dante himself about the torments of Hell, the wails of Banshees and the comings and goings of apparitions, spirits and wraiths. Not only that, but the nuns could put the heart crossways on you too with smiling tales of Limbo, Purgatory and Hell's Bells. I remember that, when one boy told the nun with some enthusiasm that the Devil stuck hot pokers up your bum, she let out a terrifying wail and ran in a great black and white blur from the room. Everyone was filled with a sense of sizzling horror and we got a substitute teacher that very afternoon.

I shuddered too one freezing mission evening, reminded by a stand-up cabaret Redemptorist that I might well for my pains go to a real place called Hell. Fire for ever and ever and ever Amen, he said, and hot pokers up the bum. And there in the pew, my feet on the pipes of the switched-off heating system, I recalled with a shiver that fatal thump and tumble into the waves. I began in sudden terror and guilt to remember strange things like the Action Man – something the grandmother disapproved of with vigour – and how I had lost it at more or less the same spot the very day before the incident with the small hammer. Another prefiguration perhaps?

It's like somethin' a wee girl would be at! the grandmother would say, you're like a sissy wee girl so you are! Would you not be better off throwing stones?

I never took any notice of her because my Action Man was by birth a football Action Man and he had fuzzy sideburns. I forget now if he had the scar on his cheek but, regardless, there wasn't a sissy bone in his body. He had a square jaw and shiny boots and could beat the shite out of anybody with his hands tied behind his back.

On this spooky Bundoran occasion he was dressed in what was called sabotage gear – black jumper, black trousers and a black woollen cap – a cross between a commando and a coalman. In one fixed-grip hand he held a flare gun and, in the other, he waved a knife which could cut the spilling guts from the belly of thrashing crocodile. In the blacks and greys of the downpour, he cut quite a dash.

This Action Man in the sabotage suit was the very man for sinking ships and raising subs. He could cut wires, bore holes, knead explosives, shine torches, slap limpet mines, paddle dinghies and peek through curtains. His Donegal assignment was to sneak into the Great Northern Hotel through a secret tunnel in the cliff and let down the tyres on all the cars in the residents' car park. It was a dangerous mission but he was well armed with a Sten gun from some other military outfit and a Luger from the days when he used to dress as a Nazi Staff Officer. I also felt that his days as a professional footballer would also stand to him in some degree.

His mission, however, was never accomplished. As I assisted in his initial absail over the edge of Roguey Rock, he slipped from my grip, tumbled, flipped and somersaulted thirty feet into the waves. Useless, he floated face down, was divebombed and pecked at by a black-headed gull and steadily and silently floated away. I think perhaps I took the whole business to be a sign of something not yet revealed and so I returned to the B & B and said nothing. He had been a Christmas present.

But then on that night of the Redemptorist mission in the creaking pew, I took these sudden memories to be a terrifying sign from the past. I had nightmares for months about Action Men with hammers in their fixed grips – all of them hacking at my skull and laughing with all the mechanical voices of a string-pull baby doll. That's guilt for you. So don't for a moment think that I was never tormented. At times it was Hell itself. The Redemptorists specialise in Hell. It's their forte, their party piece.

Odd too that my first ever exhibition after leaving art college was a series of portraits of an Action Man. It was called *Figures of Fun* and I painted full-length, face-on lifeless portraits of an Action Man in different uniforms – French Foreign Legion, Australian Bushranger, US Marine, Stormtrooper and Deep Sea Diver. It was very successful. Good review in the paper too although some city councillor wondered why the Action Man at no stage was portrayed in the uniform of any of the British regiments. There were letters to the paper and a lone picket turned up.

What added to the controversy were the other ranges of fashion and accessories that I'd had to design myself – the manufacturers never having produced an Urban Guerrilla series of their own – PLO, Basque

Separatist or any of our own local varieties with their balaclavas, sunglasses, parkas and berets.

I also did two nudes and seem to remember that these worked extremely well. As you may be aware, Action Men have strange ribcages and no genitals and I had a job explaining it all to the grandmother.

And in the paper:

DE VALERA'S VISION OF IRELAND AT LONG LAST
BECOMES A REALITY

There is a photograph of a doll known as the Barbie and it is dressed as a fabulous phenomenon known as the Irish Colleen. Rather than the standard blonde Barbie tresses, she possesses an igneous red arrangement like that of Maureen O'Hara (or was it Maureen O'Sullivan?), Mary Kate Danaher or Jane? John Wayne or Johnny Weissmuller? *The Quiet Man* or *Tarzan*? Maurice Walsh or Edgar Rice Burroughs? No matter.

She sports a lace hat, a green dress with yet more lace and on her two brown feet – green shoes with inhuman toes. The paper points out that she has a jabot collar fastened with a shamrock button. A nut-brown maid as white as a ghost.

The accompanying photograph is of an awful, spindly, sexless, beaming figment of somebody's lack of imagination and you would think at once of the tourist dishcloth. The Irish Barbie Doll – smiling at me out the paper – barefoot at the crossroads – retailing for between fifteen and twenty pounds.

33

I near boke and begin angrily to mix my paints – greens and reds.

And so I painted a demon John Hinde postcard donkey being led by the nose by a naked Action Man. That done, I kicked it around the room, put my fist through it, sat down in the corner and got full on neat frozen vodka from the duty-free at Prague. It was miraculous and pure.

THE LIVES OF THE SAINTS

Bundoran and always it lashed. Always it teemed and we would be confined to B & B or caravan – looking out the windows like animals in a zoo where people had long since stopped coming. Sometimes we would force ourselves and step out into the downpour and deserted streets and nip from shop to shop – stand in the doorways and stare at the bubbling drains. It was a town with no light and the only real comfort came from the cosy heat of rotating chickens in the window of the Bonne Tuck.

Bundoran was always July and July was when the father got the fortnight's holidays from the meat factory. As I've said before, he never let on what exactly he did for a living but I think I knew in my heart that it involved killing the poor moo-moos. Anyway, there was always some silent darkness about the whole thing and wouldn't it be a rare irony now if the father's job had been to whack the moo-moos on the head with a hammer? How much do you bet?

In total, sodden misery we would hover around the amusements and try to shoot side-on ducks or win something on the slot machines. I would spend my pocket money on a game which made me a submariner taking pot-shots at convoys. It was all sonar, explosions and racket and I'm sure the father would have given all the money in Ireland to be back among the moo-moos and the guts. The only thing I ever got him to do in the amusements was to squeeze the iron horns of a bull's head in order to test his strength. And he broke it in bits. It takes a strong wrist to kill a moo-moo.

I could go on about this at length but I don't want to allow the inevitable misery of a rain-lashed holiday to detract from the incredible magic of the place when the sun shone and I took to burying my skinny sunburnt legs in the sand. I was for-ever burying things – bottles, sandwiches, shells, stones, shoes, hubcaps – but by far the strangest and most solemn interment ever conducted by me was the secretive occasion when I buried a shoplifted holy statue – the Holy Infant of Prague – just at the tideline – upright, beatific and serene. If the grandmother had known about that she'd have had my life.

It was during those wet bolts from shop to shop that I began to get religion. The windows were full of all manner of broc and garbage but amid all of the souvenirs and shells and plastic leprechauns there were the holy water fonts, the statues and the holy pictures of Jesus, Mary and Joseph and all the saints in Heaven.

Some things were made of plaster, some of metal and some of luminous plastic. Some of the pictures were in 3-D and some of the plastic statues of Mary doubled as holy water bottles with blue screw-top crowns. Great presents too for the grandmother and her home-baking house was full of the stuff.

It was the statues of the saints which fascinated me the most and I began to collect them like my own private army. They were like Marvel superheroes – each with special gifts and uniforms and so, out of total drenched boredom, I became, for a brief time, a ten-year-old religious maniac. I gathered the saints around me and relaxed.

Saint Anthony of Padua, Saint Martin de Porres, Saint Jude, Saint Patrick, Saint Michael, Saint Oliver Plunkett and, of course, the Holy Infant of Prague. In those days I thought the Child of Prague was a child from Prague but only recently I discovered that the little man who had been standing sentry on my windowsill was in fact Jesus himself. That's a whole other story and my bizarre relationship with this little statue will become clear as we progress – but first some very necessary hagiography based primarily on my recollection of the granny's only book – *The Lives of the Saints.*

Saint Martin de Porres: Born Lima, Peru, in 1579. Illegitimate son of Anna Velasquez and John de Porres, Knight of the Order of Alcantara. Usually depicted as a fine-looking man in Dominican robes holding a brush and a loaf of bread. At his feet, a little dish and there, feeding together, you will find a cat, a dog, a mouse and a bird. A great man for the animals and they were equally fond of him.

Always charitable, he worked hard for the poor of

Lima. Much loved and there was great joy when he was canonised in 1962. Because of the blackness of his skin, he was often referred to in Fermanagh homes as Sugar Ray Robinson – a reference to a skilled boxer of old. Patron Saint of Barbers.

Saint Jude: 1st first-century apostle and Patron Saint of Hopeless Cases. Also known as Thaddeus and the brother of James the Less. The very man for examinations, driving tests and crazy enterprises. It is said that nobody ever asked Saint Jude for anything because he was confused with Judas and so whenever anybody did invoke him, he was delighted to assist. More than happy as a matter of fact. Often seen thanked in the pages of the quality press. Usually depicted holding a club which was the cruel instrument of his martyrdom.

Saint Oliver Plunkett: Born Loughcrew, County Meath, in 1629. Archbishop of Armagh. Smart man and smooth operator, finally arrested after false allegations by a rum playboy called Titus Oates and brought to Newgate. Tried for treason by Sir Francis Pemberton and executed at Tyburn in 1681. The gory tale of his hanging, drawing and quartering is much loved by schoolboys of primary school age. Body is now at Downside Abbey in Somerset and head in Drogheda. Canonised in 1976. Clatter of football teams named after him.

Saint Anthony of Padua: Born Lisbon, Portugal, in

1193 of a rich and well-to-do family. A Franciscan and heavy teacher of theology which got him the title of the Hammer of the Heretics. Often seen preaching to fish and this reminds me of the many long hours I spent at the loughshore in the company of coots and waterhens, watching the bream rolling and the fry skittering. Also seen holding the host up in front of a donkey and this I do not understand. My statue, however, showed Saint Anthony in his Franciscan robes holding a book and a lily and with the child Jesus sitting up on the open book.

The very man if you lost anything – a quick prayer and he could locate something at the drop of a hat. The grandmother would, however, cast scorn on this notion saying –

Do you not think Saint Anthony has enough to do without having to look for the Auntie Mary's lipstick?

Point of information. He once recovered a faulty boomerang for me. Buried at Padua in 1231 and can-onised a year later. Among his relics is his incorrupt tongue.

Saint Joseph: Joiner, husband of Mary, foster-father of Jesus, dreamer of dreams. Went the whole way from Nazareth to Bethlehem with a heavily pregnant wife without sorting out a place to stay in advance but was nevertheless a very skilled joiner and rarely used a nail. Patron saint of fathers, procurators, bursars and all manual workers, particularly joiners. See the Protevangelium of James and *The History of Joseph the*

Carpenter (a Greek work of the fifth–sixth century). Not to be confused with Joseph of Arimathea or the Flying Friar himself – Joseph of Cupertino who used to zoom about the church helping workmen – carrying hammers, planks and chisels up to the ceiling. A handy boy about the house

Saint Patrick: Hail Glorious Saint Patrick! Dear Saint of our Isle. Shamrocks, snakes and lighting big fires!

Saint Michael: Sword-fighting, sky-blue, Devil-hating, angelic hard man. Celestial bouncer with a school called after him. Tough cookie.

It is quite extraordinary how much I remember of the saints and their lives but then again it was the granny's only book.

Who would be your favourite saint, Granny?

Saint Gerard Majella, she would say, and Saint Maria Goretti and Saint Bernadette and Saint Jude and Saint Catherine of Siena and Saint Bridget and Saint Ignatius and Saint Molaise and Saint Malachy and Saint Martin and Saint Anthony and Saint Joseph and Saint James and Saint Basil and Saints Perpetua and Felicity and Saint Anastasia and Saint John Vianni and Saint Barnabas and . . .

So she needed them about her and I need my things about me too. The easel is set up, the canvas is chosen, the brushes are laid out and caressed in turn. Each and every tube of paint is lovingly considered. An old tube of Prussian blue that I've had for ten years

– bought in London on a summer evening of brandy and ginger – an old tube of titanium white which I nearly used up completely in the Elvis portrait and so on and so on. I could go on until the cows have come home and gone out again and maybe that's what I'm doing now. Getting my things about me. Getting in the mood. Footerin'. No sense in just barging into it all ramstam. The Roguey pickaxe, that whole Prague business, the unfortunate demise of head-the-ball and how the people came in droves. It's all kind of convoluted – not at all like painting a yellow coot or a hurtling horse. Not at all like the barnacled ochre and green of a lumbering whale crushed by its own weight on sharp and sedimentary rocks. Certainly not as clear to me as a full-length portrait of the King or a scandalous childhood memory of a palaeontologist going arse-over-tit into the green Atlantic sea. Like a sack o' spuds.

And so, all of the above saints, plus the Holy Infant of Prague, were arrayed on the polished dressing-table. Outside, the Bundoran rain bucketed down and the holidaymakers all ran for cover. Lying on the terraces and ridges of the lemon guesthouse quilt I thought about the palaeontologist and how I'd have to keep my mouth shut for the rest of my life. It was no joke.

THE COCKROACH

And then, out of the blue, it was on the phone –
squeezing its way into my Bundoran reverie with a
high-pitched ringing and a blethering voice –

Good afternoon. It's Clive Ratcliff here of Firecracker Films. Clive Ratcliff Firecracker Films.

He had that voice – either English or else pretending he wasn't Irish – employing the mid-Irish
sea cadences of shuttler. Like those long-winded
frauds who inhabit a makey-up province of career
and success where townland carries no clout and
relics of decency are sold in the market place –
Aldergrove, Heathrow, the London Underground
and the far-from-where-you-were-reared restaurants
of Kensington. He also had a touch of that US uplift at
the end of a sentence that makes everything seem like
a question you couldn't be bothered answering.

The Cockroach was making no real sense but
was clearly after something. His prolonged self-
introduction was vague and twisting and clearly
intended to creat an impression – something about
Giacometti, a new *space* somewhere in town, a
retrospective, studio time, projects, concepts, how
very busy he was and some implied suggestion that
I was obliged to listen to him –

Where did you get my number? I asked cutting him off mid-spiel.

He had no answer that I could understand.

What is your name again?

Clive Ratcliff Firecracker Films, he said solemnly. Clive Ratcliff Firecracker Films.

I faked a lack of recognition even though I knew damn well who he was. Every painter in the country had heard of him and we had tipped each other off to have nothing ever to do with him because Clive Ratcliff The Cockroach was the worst kind of cockroach – a cockroach who worked in television. He was a vampire, a leech – an empty vessel that needed to be filled by the ideas of others. This way he fancied he might live for ever in the credits. He was a virus, a parasite and a pest and he needed a good kick in the arse.

Please do not phone me again, I said.

His mental receiver was faulty.

I'll give you another little bell, he said as if trying to console me about something, when you're not so busy.

Listen! I protested calmly, I'm not in the least bit busy. In fact, I was sitting contentedly on my backside thinking about swingboats and bumpin' cars when you . . .

An inadvertent cue –

Marvellous! he spluttered, marvellous, yes they're absolutely marvellous. I have a huge interest in old fairground attractions myself. In fact, it's something of an obsession. Actually, my great-uncle operated the merry-go-round at Torquay. Marvellous carved wooden ponies – I always thought of them as those magnificent horses in the Piazza San Marco. They are so real! So lifelike! Remarkable musculature and movement and . . .

I experienced a sudden flashback of a palaeontologist tumbling down into the waves like a bag full of himself and I hung up.

I was fit to be tied. Horses no less! Obsessed with fairground attractions he said! If I'd told him I'd been thinking about Christmas he'd have claimed that his great-uncle was Santy Claus. I'd run into people like him before all right – they'd do or say anything just to get in with you. Tell you lies from start to finish! Fantasyland! Living in detached villas in some secluded corner of cuckooland – close to all amenities and bugger all to do with themselves all day except annoy people like me. I was feeling all of a sudden murderous. Vodka. Vodka. Vodka. And only vodka would do.

And I still had the hammer too. Oh, I had it all right! It hadn't been decommissioned yet! Of course, the grandmother thought that I chucked it into the swelling Atlantic sea seconds after the event but the truth of it is that I kept it concealed about my person for a fortnight or so and then transferred it to a secluded corner of the toy-box – Lego, Airfix, Powerballs, shuttlecocks, Spud-Gun, darts, rubber snakes, vampire teeth, plastic handcuffs and a dead man's clothes – the unfilled boots of an Action Man lost in action.

44

What's the rule? Mind your tool. And periodically I would take the hammer out and place it some distance away and stare at it with great conviction. The initials P. M. on the handle – Prime Minister, Post Meridian. I think I was trying to arouse some kind of guilt in myself but no such feeling ever emerged. The fact is that I had gotten away with it and even if I was to go to straight to the Guards, the RUC, Interpol or the Redemptorists right now, nobody would believe me anyway. They would think it a fairy story –

Aye surely, they would say. Bundoran you say? July you say? Aye surely.

More vodka. To tell you the truth I never give the palaeontologist much thought – other than to occasionally review the action. The back of the head. The grain of the handle. The sudden violence. Of course, I have often asked myself the obvious questions. Was I some kind of psycho? And if I was – why nothing similar since apart from a couple of incidents and the sadistic frazzling of beetles using only a magnifying glass and the glorious sun of a Twelfth Fortnight? And the big question – was I likely to commit such violence ever again? After all, sometimes I can get very ratty.

And then, strangely, I would ask myself whether or not it had happened at all? Maybe it was all a fairy story in the wind-up? Maybe the grandmother was doting and had imagined the whole thing and somewhere along the line I had begun to believe it myself? Or maybe it was me who was deluded?

But in the end-up I always thought it wise to

believe and after all (despite my initial paranoia) I had an unshakeable faith in the grandmother. All I had to do was keep the mouth shut and she would plug up the leaky family boat should the need arise. We would all be as right as rain. Absolut. Stoli. A Smirnoff miniature.

My pals the saints never offered much advice. Aware and all as I was that they had come from a background of guilt and repentance, this, despite the ethos of teacher, Church and State, was a sensation I seemed unable to properly experience. Only in works of literature did I detect people allegedly tormented with a thing called guilt. But not me. I could sleep perfectly well in my bed at night thank you very much.

The above notwithstanding, my religious mania phase continued unchecked between the ages of seven and ten and a half. The saints continued to form a protective ring around me and the Holy Infant of Prague, despite a brief period of headlessness, remained intact on windowsill sentry duty thanks be to Sellotape and gluey glue. The grandmother continued to be an influence and it is perhaps worth noting that, once a year, herself and myself thumbed it to a place called Knock in the County of Mayo.

Now a class of theme park for Catholics, Knock in those days was a more primitive affair. A gable wall, holy water and the faithful kneeling in a murmuring, freezing huddle. They watched that wall like they were at a picture-house where the projector had temporarily broken down. No question but it would start up again and they would not miss any of the miraculous action when it did – pick the story up from where it had left off in 1879.

Mary the Mother of God (and others) are said to have appeared on the gable wall in question. Nothing was said but the locals were understandably well shook. Word spread, cures happened, redundant crutches were hung up on the wall and the cult began. The grandmother was particularly disposed to this kind of thing and made the pilgrimage once a year, reciting about two dozen rosaries on the round trip – the whole thing in aid of the bad back.

And often there are dreams of the grandmother. Many memories and visitations.

Myself and herself (halfway through her first decade of her first rosary) are standing on the Sligo Road and out with the thumb. Almost immediately, and perhaps miraculously, we get a lift in a silver Cortina. The grandmother is immediately jumpy and just before we slide together into the back seat, she grabs me by the bones of my elbow and whispers ferociously –

Say nothin', son! You wouldn't know who you'd be talkin' to these days! Not a word out of you! And don't let on where we're going either!

I can't really see the driver apart from the back of his head. His hair is short and shaved close on the nape of his neck which sprouts with several explosive spots. He possibly wears a weak moustache.

Where are yis headin'? he asks, examining us in the rear-view mirror.

Say nothin'! hisses the grandmother, he's out of the Barracks! I know by the cut of him!

Our driver hears and nervously mutters that he is only going as far as Sligo and will that do us? I say that it will surely and the grandmother viciously digs her elbow into my ribs –

For God's sake, Granny! You can't thumb a lift and not tell the man where you're going!

God, take care of us and protect us, she mutters.

The driver shifts in his seat –

Are you on your way to Knock, missus?

The grandmother gasps and makes a sudden move to get out of car –

Oh, sweet Mother of God! We'll all be lifted!

Missus! Missus! Houl on! I was there myself last weekend! The place was packed so it was!

The driver seems to smile a nervous holy smile and the grandmother is immediately satisfied of her ground. On the minute, she ostentatiously whips out the beads and begins to recite Hail Marys, Our Fathers and Glory Bes. Our pimply driver is silently compelled by years of ritual to answer the second half of each prayer and then piously give the lead when his turn comes. Prayers are temporarily suspended for UDR checkpoints and for some Scotch regiment at the border itself but are immediately resumed with even greater fervour once over the ramp, over the spikes, across the chain and into the State. As the car pulls into Sligo they are singing 'Hail Queen of Heaven' in perfect tight harmony.

From Sligo we get a lift to Castlebar with a carload

48

of nuns who are already lamenting the rosary and so, naturally enough, the grandmother is delighted with herself although I myself am beginning to feel a bit carsick with the repetition of it all. The nuns themselves are young and giddy and I think to myself that they'd much rather be going to Butlin's than rattling along the sodden roads of Mayo meditating on the Sorrowful, Joyful and Glorious Mysteries – but then a vow is a vow and the nuns are tough women.

In no time at all we appear in Knock. The grandmother thanks the sisters and they all giggle and at once seem to vanish into the air –

Grand lassies them nuns – bit of life about them, says the grandmother.

There is already a big crowd at the gable wall and myself and the grandmother edge in among them. There follows more praying and much focusing on the bricks. Around us a thousand bodies, twisted in pain and silent anguish, faithfully await the miracle to come. I am confused and upset and realise that I am very young and know nothing much about anything.

Right, son! C'mon! whispers the grandmother suddenly, we'll go back by Donegal!

In no time at all we are back on the road waving down lorries with our sanctified thumbs. We have to stop at every well and holy place – every grotto, stone and fairy thorn.

And always these dreams of the grandmother. The memories and the visitations. And tortured in the morning, I awake with a dry mouth and a pumping heart on the wooden Jackson Pollock boards of the studio floor and think of the granny through the gaps in the sore head.

You're like the Wreck of the Hesperus, the grandmother used to say when I was a cub. A strange handshake. We'll hardly know ourselves. Handsel money. Damn the bit. God bless the work. Not the day or yesterday. Innocent as sin. Divil the hate. Hilt nor Hare. As true as God. Desperate to the World. God take care of us.

These were the mysterious and magic words of the grandmother – devoted to cures, moon-gazing, plant-gathering and fairies – all governing her life as much as any of the Ten Commandments or the numerous and fearsome rules of the Church to which she claimed a vague allegiance – hydrolatry or not.

And that time we thumbed it into Donegal – Belleek, Ballyshannon, Donegal Town, Mountcharles, Killybegs, Kilcar and on to Slieve League and the townland of Rinnakilla overlooking Teelin Harbour. There in the middle of whins and cowshite there is a hole in the ground – Tobar na mBán Naomh – the Well of the Holy Women – and the grandmother was certainly one of them.

She immediately knelt and, using a delf cup there for the purpose, she scooped up the water from the well and bathed her face in it. She poured more of it over my head and then, with delicate and elaborate modesty, she managed to rub cupfuls of this healing water into her bad back. Two lemonade bottles were then filled and passed to me. This rigmarole completed, she maintained that she was feeling like a youngster again and that the Well of the Holy Women beat all.

A rough kind of shrine stood no distance away – a drystone wall enclosure with an old cross on top of it. In the wall itself there was a little grotto crammed full of objects left by the faithful – statues, miraculous medals, scapulas and of course a multitude of Infants of Prague. It was at this place that the grandmother started to act in a particularly strange fashion.

There were three stones lying at the foot of the shrine and for some reason that she could never explain to me, she always, without fail, picked each one up in turn and passed it around her body three times. She then kissed it and replaced it. When she had done this to her satisfaction and supervised my own amateur performance, she then emptied the contents of her pockets into the grotto – safety pins, thrupenny bits, a washer –

Why are you doing that, Granny? I asked.

Just, she answered.

What is it anyway? I asked the grandmother.

It's a holy well, son, she replied.

Do the priests ever come here?

Of course, she couldn't have cared less whether the priests came or not. It had nothing to do with the priests. Saint Patrick and his big fire my eye! The patron saint was wasting his time as far as the grandmother was concerned and both herself and himself knew it. Off to Mass on a First Friday one minute and people calling to the house for a lock of her hair to cure the whooping cough the next. Seventh daughter of a seventh daughter. I see the moon, the moon sees me.

It was a Bloody Mary for breakfast and The Cockroach on the blower. He had picked a bad time for the early-morning call –

Good morning! I hope I haven't disturbed you. Clive Ratcliff Firecracker Films here again. Just to follow up on our conversation last evening and to run a few ideas past you. I am very, very busy at the moment but as regards your project . . .

My project! Correct me if I'm wrong, Mister Ratcliff Fuckin' Firescheister Films but didn't I tell you never to ring me again?

Oh yes indeed, marvellous! I appreciate that you're rather busy. I mean I'm very busy myself with paper-work and meetings and I have to go to the mainland tomorrow to meet with some people from . . .

Mister Ratcliff, I said calmly, beginning in deliberate tones but soon freewheeling, you are a fraudulent, two-faced, useless, talentless, valueless, bloodsucking bastard – and if you ever contact me again you will die a cruel and unusual death and you will not live to see your next miserable, hateful production. I swear to you, Mister Ratcliff, I will actually kill you. You are the slimy embodiment of all that I despise – all that is wrong with the opportunistic, false, unscrupulous, corrupt, shabby, double-dealing, hypocritical and time-serving milieu in which you prosper. I have no desire to be a part of it and

I certainly have no desire to go anywhere near a charlatan like you! You will not sell my soul like an old horse to some commissioning editor who can't even pronounce Ballinamallard! You and your mainland and your budgets and your network strands! Fuck away off!

As I hung up I sighed in exhausted acceptance that it might take a stake through the heart to stop a cockroach vampire like him. I knew also that if I ever heard his sleekit wee voice again I would have to retrieve the sleeping hammer from the toy-box. Seriously. I was quite serious. I'd hammer in the morning.

BE PREPARED

And so much for the childhood influences of hon-
oured grandmother, invisible mother, moo-moo-
slaughtering father and model saints with model
lives. Outside of all that, I formed most of my
own notions in these formative years virtuously free
of the usually pervasive influences of Church, school
and children's programmes on the BBC. *Vision On*,
Blue Peter and so on – endless palaver that had my
peers buggered entirely.

I was, in most things, singular and was, for all
intents and purposes, an only child (apart from the
mysterious, absent and unmentionable sister). Perhaps
it is quite inevitable that an only child develops
this independence of thought in the early years?
Quite inevitable too is the uncontrollable and, at
times, spectacular imagination – all part of that very
necessary capacity to amuse yourself. Happy as the
day's long playing away there on the floor. That I had
a gruesome murder under my belt I'm sure played no
small part either.

I'm certain sure also that it was precisely because
of my status as an only child that I became acquainted
so early and to such an advanced level with the
disciplines of palaeontology, hagiography, botany,

coal-shade lepping, pike-fishing, archery and ball-juggling. The grandmother said that I was a brainbox.

I'm sure too that the reason I turned to painting as a way of life was all to do with my solo nature. I had always preferred the lonely pursuit to the communal and so I took to the brush and the turpentine. I dabbed and it became my life.

Now and again I made an effort at more social pursuits like rounders and football but could never take any pleasure in the hatred provoked whenever you missed a sitter or let the ball go between your legs. Others, the buckteeth cousins for instance, thrived on the ritual torture of it and there was no surprise in that – them being twisted and taking after the parents.

Any wonder then that I took to painting when all efforts at the group thing proved disastrous – like the short-lived gangs we formed at primary school at the prompting of comic books like *Warlord* or *Fireball*?

Most of that period was to do with self-defence techniques and how to survive in the wild – wandering the hills with a tobacco tin survival kit full of nuts, raisins, sticking plasters, chocolate buttons and safety pins to be used as fish hooks in case of emergency. In those days I was usually ready for anything – compass, water bottle, binoculars and a penknife that wouldn't cut butter.

One Saturday afternoon, against my better judgement, I joined up with a horde of other members of the Warlord Club or the Fireball Club or whatever it was, and began to survive on the side of a hill overlooking the Barracks. There must have been about a dozen of us like rabid apostles assembling, unsure of our purpose and gazing out over the wet slates of the town.

And so, armed with sticks and branches and survival kits we began to run and circle and roll and crawl and leap and climb and swing – charging like maniacs through briars and brambles and slicing at the cow-parsley with our sally scimitars. The totally deranged among our number silently shinned up and down lamp-posts and telegraph poles and seemed quite content. Happy as the day was long.

Our purposelessness was both evident and embarrassing but nevertheless provided sufficient provocation to bring a local and fearsome gang leader out of his hallway. He felt the gut-need to defend his own dubious territory and within seconds he had reared up in our midst like a short monster from Hell. He spat out the most terrifying and ferocious language imaginable and immediately and as one we all stood back – making widening concentric circles of our absences.

I'll friggin' kill yis! I'll friggin kill every last hoor of yis! Bastards! Bastards! I'll friggin' well friggin' kill all of yis! Frig! Frig off! Frig! Frig off! Frig!

And then with outrageous energy the dervish, hurricane, whirlpool beast suddenly uprooted a young rowan tree and began to flail it wildy about his head in a very vicious circle – the red berries flying in all directions. Again we stepped back into a wider circle. Chromatography. A ripple effect.

Our alleged gang was wary because our sudden foe had obviously studied closely the Bruce Lee films at the Ritz and was therefore a formidable and dangerous enemy. *Enter the Dragon* had been on that week but the granny wouldn't let me go because, according to her, it was an X and there were bad women in it from Red China.

As our crazed enemy scythed away with the young tree, another lesson was then suddenly learnt. Before I had worked out exactly what to do in these unbalancing circumstances, the rest of our brave gang had evaporated, dispersed and dismissed themselves in apathy and disarray. One or two even went off traitorously and all pals with the enemy. The grandmother had indeed predicted that it would end in tears and so I swallowed the raw bitterness of that first betrayal and took myself off for a dander. On my own-ee-o. I thought about Judas and how it would have been better for him if he had not been born.

And away I went to look at the herons' nests in the hope of provoking the boke from above. It's a fact that a disturbed heron will discourage visitors from the trunk of his tree by regurgitating the sushi all over them – bad enough if you're ready for it – but imagine the sensation of stepping through the undergrowth and suddenly feeling a half-digested eel slap down on your shoulder from a great height. Not the pleasantest, but I love the herons even so – they are solitary, silent and patient and yet capable of great screeching, frog-stabbing and precision-boking. Their feet, I have also observed, must never get cold.

Ornithological interlude:

The heron or *Ardea cinera* as smart men call them belong to the family Ardeidae as does the bittern – *Botaurus stellaris* – the yellow one of poetic fame. The sky-hanging heron is a resident bird and when we were children we called them cranes – but not the same crane your father might pretend to be when attempting to feed you creamed rice with a jaggy fork. Herons stretch themselves upright in the rushes and half the time you can't see them at all.

And in the paper:

FIVE HUNDRED CUE FOR MIRACLE

A temple in Belfast. There's a statue of an elephant and it is drinking milk! It's Ganesh the elephant god of wisdom and he's drinking away. People are coming with cartons full. They say it means that a great soul has come on earth. Apparently it started in India and thousands of people out there are witnessing the miracle.

And then things took a very bad turn when a letter arrived from The Cockroach. He clearly hadn't heard me right. His tortured communication amounted to one long sentence and it enraged me so much that I put my foot though the already busted sofa and smashed three out of three expectant picture frames.

Reading the letter, I could just hear the sleekit little whine of him.

> *Good news I have just returned to the province after a very busy trip to the mainland where I have been discussing you're [sic] film with the commissioning editor who seems to agree that you are an interesting subject for a film even though he admits he is not familiar with your work or with the province but even so he is excited at the possibility of fliming [sic] you in your natural enviroment [sic] of the lakelands where we can get some exterior shots of water, birds and sunsets, and speaking of which I suggest we meet tomorrow evening when I would be delighted to buy you a light supper and discuss any difficulties you might have with the project so far.*
> *Yours in art,*
> *Clive C. Ratcliff Firecracker Films Ltd*

The Cockroach clearly believed me to be as stupid as he was himself and I found that at once both hurtful and unforgivable. After all, we all need to be taken seriously. Not taking yourself too seriously is one thing but not being taken seriously by a balloon like him was a different thing entirely.

Like in the Boy Scouts. That was another whole episode! Sitting around a damp campfire singing –

> *You'll never get to heaven with Brigitte Bardot*
> *'Cos Brigitte Bardot is going below.*

I didn't know who Bridget whateverhername was but the grandmother told me that she was a bad woman and that they were all like that out foreign in Paris. But I sang the song anyway to try to make the most out of the forced jollity and all that camaraderie bullshite –

> *There was a man who had a dog*
> *And Bingo was his name.*

We tied things together with sheepshanks and reef knots, we paced-off, stood to attention, stood at ease, saluted and pitched leaky tents in wet fields. I was the leader of Bull(shite) Patrol and whenever I would order some wee skitter to go and get water or gather firewood he would pay no attention to me and tell me to get it my so-and-so self. And best of it all, I couldn't have cared less anyway.

We made strange Masonic signs with three fingers and learnt a thing called the Scout Law – Loyal, Trustworthy, Helpful, Friendly, Courteous and Kind, Obedient, Cheerful and Thrifty, Brave, Pure, God's glory in mind. And we promised something about keeping this law with our hand on some flag or other.

Anyway, on this particular pre-pubescent, neckerchiefed night we were camping on a snow-covered mountain overlooking the meat factory and its conveyor-belt of guts – fondue set, clock radio, cuddly toy – and the cheerful, brave and trustworthy campfire conclave took a bit of a turn when the ratboys began to talk excitedly of their alleged exploits.

One had been to a disco on his holidays in Bundoran and he had snoggered [sic] a girl. Another had similarly snoggered [sic] a girl behind the Orange Hall and someone else (while snoggering [sic] a girl) had been attacked by six hard lads and he had busted them all armed only with a bin lid and steel toecaps.

None of it was believable and soon I was bored, cold and wondering why I was on a snowy mountainside putting a match to smuggled Zip firelighters and in a position of vague responsibility for the wimpy, red-faced and out-of-proportion basket cases of Bull(shite) Patrol. I began to think about Sophia Loren.

I bet you've never snoggered a girl? squeaked one of them in challenge.

Go and get more wood for the fire! I commanded.

Bugger off! he snapped. You'll not order me about!

I'll give you a quare slap in the mouth!

You touch me and I'll get me brother for you!

G'won home to your mother fuckye!

Then the rest of them started to jeer and give me the fingers. And what did I do, only lose the rag altogether and pick up a large curly-ended mallet and leap to my damp feet to glare through the flames at my ratboy persecutors. A sudden liberated rage consumed me and I felt released and fearsome. They did not seem one bit afraid, however, and one or two sniggered behind their wrists.

See the next man who laughs at me! See this mallet! I'll friggin' brain him with it!

Little did they know and I felt at once both powerful and capable, confident that my face was red in the heat of anger and campfire. I hoped too that my raging eyes were burning red and I took pleasure in the satisfying heaviness of the mallet. Old grain-handled feelings returned.

Ah sit down, you big tube! someone whined.

I'm warnin' you, I shouted with venom, I'll friggin' kill somebody. Frig! Frig Off! Frig!

But unlike the mad dog with the rowan tree – nobody took me seriously and there was a long blood-pumping silence. It lasted moment after moment until their gaping faces suddenly began to crack and their awful laughter began to rise once again through the flames. Soon they were laughing out loud – laughing until they could hardly breathe. Somebody screamed that they were about to wet themselves and then they got hysterical – choking and coughing and near-boking with laughter. I thought for a moment that I would cease their cackling with one swift blow but instead I said to myself (employing the word for the second time) fuck this for a game of darts and I flung the mallet hard into the belly of the fire where it sent a million fiery sparks into the smoky sky.

But there was no trauma. There were no scars. Quite the opposite in fact – water off a duck's back and an epiphanic apathy suddenly licking around my bones. I hissed a long, lazy spit through my teeth and waited for the fire to hiss it back to me. And then, satisfied with the sound, I walked off through the blackness of bramble and ditch.

It said in the handbook that a Scout tries to become a saint. It said that the best way to end a campfire singsong was with 'Salve Regina'. It said that biting your fingernails was disgusting and that you had to be careful passing an axe. It had said many things. *Imprimi Potest of Joannes Carolus Archiep. Dublinen.*

I stepped through the calm of receding squealing and within five minutes I was confidently and powerfully at home beneath my own quilt – all remaining desire for merit badges and sainthood gone like the sparky smoke. Late that night I could still hear Bullshite Patrol singing away to themselves on the snowy bank of whins –

> *The German soldiers crossed the Rhine*
> *Parlez-vous!*

That was me and the Scouts. I deserted.

And in the paper:

VIRGIN MARY LOST

Kent Police have appealed for the owner of a three-foot-high statue of Mary to come forward. It was found in a car park. Just appeared there. *Salve Regina.*

And this one:

It would appear that a chicken fell from the tenth floor of a tower block and hit a blind man on the head. And now he can see. Cured him.

I spent much of the day cleaning old brushes and working out just how exactly The Cockroach would swim with the fishes.

THE CHILD OF PRAGUE

I have mentioned on several occasions a certain sanctified figurine that I now feel may need further and overdue elucidation. I am strongly of this view because I have recently encountered educated Englishmen, one of them a well-known commentator on the arts and popular culture, who knew nothing about it whatsoever. I am referring to the Child of Prague – the little man for whom the grandmother had always nurtured an excessive devotion.

The Child or Infant of Prague, the Bambino di Praga, the pražské Jezulátko is an object of intense veneration housed at the Carmelite Church of Panna Maria Vítězná on Karmelitská in the City of Praha in the Czech Republic – the former Czechoslovakia. I have seen it there myself.

Travellers in Ireland will be familiar with the sight of this little man perched upon the windowsills of bedrooms and kitchens – often headless and regarded by some to be quite powerless until properly so decapitated. You will also hear tell of the Bambino being placed overnight in the wet and dripping gardens of believers on the eve of a wedding in order to secure clement weather for the big day. And many will contend that the Infant of Prague never fails to intercede with nature on behalf of bride and groom. In fact, I've seen it done myself in Ballycastle.

First some facts. The little man is a forty-seven-centimetre-tall wax sculpture of the child Jesus. If, however, you were to ask anybody in possession of a Child of Prague who exactly the statue represented, I'd put real money on it that very few would be fit to tell you. In any case the little man – the Bambino di Praga – is now a cult – part of a long cultic tradition of the Baby Jesus. (I refer you here to the usual representation of Saint Anthony of Padua, the Hammer of the Heretics.)

This cult of Christ's childhood gathered pace in the Baroque period and was linked to the visions of Theresa of Avila. A number of sculptures were found in her country of origin and it was one of these very Spanish sculptures that ended up in Prague. It is widely believed that the Infant came from a monastery somewhere between Cordoba and Seville and that it comes to us from Isabella Manrique de Lara y Mendoza.

She presented the little man as a wedding gift to her daughter Maria Manrique de Lara when she married a Czech nobleman called Vratislav of Pernštejn. In later years, the little man became a wedding present once more as Maria's daughter Polyxena married a Czech big-wheel called Vilém of Rožmberk. Later, Polyxena married again, this time the Supreme Chancellor of the Czech Kingdom whose name was Zdeněk Vojtěch of Lobkowice and when he died,

Polyxena presented the little man to the Order of the Barefooted Carmelites in Malá Strana.

And so the cult developed. Prior Ludvik put the statue in the oratory and as the fortunes of the monastery turned for the better, the wee man got all the credit. But even so, once all the young novices so fond of the Infant had headed off for Munich, the extent of devotion decreased. Then, in 1631, the Saxons invaded Prague and plundered the Carmelite Monastery. Tossed the place.

Eventually, these Saxon yobs were beaten back and run out, but too late for the Child and in 1633 the Crown withdrew all financial support for the convent. Then the Swedes invaded and the statue disappeared altogether until 1638 when Nicholas Schockwilerg arrived from Luxembourg and the cult began to expand again. Miracles were attributed. And yet more miracles attributed, And such was the reverence in which the little man was held during the Swedish Siege of Prague that he became a great favourite with the Czech nobility who, fair play to them, gave bucketloads of money to the Church.

Then the cute Carmelites caught themselves on and decided to exhibit the Bambino to the public and eventually it was placed in the Chapel of the Holy Rood. The Emperor Ferdinand himself came to kneel at the wee man's feet and he even donated forty candles. All sorts of big knobs continued to be very fond of the Child and they gave many gifts and presents to the Church – the Lady Febronia of Pernštejn, Lady Brunetti, John Conrad of Altendorf, the Count and Countess Kolowrat, the Earls of Hammond and Downshire.

One Colonel Kappy then persuaded General Königsmark to issue a warrant of protection for the Bambino as requested by the Carmelites. They were well connected the nuns. Even King Gustav of Sweden came to see the wee man and give him a present. Then they all started. Bernard Ignatius of Martinic gave him the gold crown with its pearls and precious stones. The King of Spain hung the cloak around his shoulders to mark the conferment of the Order of The Golden Fleece. And his wee house was built by Elizabeth Constance of Potting. *Eremitorium dulcissimi pueri Iesu.* The orb was swiped in 1733.

The whole thing really took off when Emerich a St Stephano wrote a book called *Pragerisches Gross und Klein* in 1736 (translated into Czech in 1749). He told the whole story and so it was that our man got so popular. More miracles. All the fancy clothes coming from all over the world to dress him up. And then when porcelain copies were made in Meissen, they wouldn't break the mould and before you could say boo, the wee man began to appear in all the churches of Malá Strana and all over Prague and Bohemia. Copies eventually made their way to France and to Poland and on to Asia where the fame of the little man spread. And so to Ireland and the farmhouse windowsills of Donegal and Fermanagh. The Bambino di Praga. Headless weatherman. Buried in Bundoran. And never fails.

DNA

Naturally I jilted The Cockroach. Stood him up and left him to enjoy his fried Brie on his lonesome. I spent the evening painting – working on a landscape from memory. I wasn't happy with it but I believed I might be on to something for the next time – a wellstead I remember seeing on Malin Head planked right in the centre of one of those rectangular hillside fields that seem to be hanging out to dry.

That night I dreamt that The Cockroach, media parasite from hell, had finally got his head in his hands and had been discovered in four separate pieces inside his own filing cabinet. Great words like torso appeared for over a week in the pages of the *Belfast Telegraph* and his secretary was reported to have laughed uproariously.

That dream preceded some terrific creative activity the following day. The landscape was abandoned and other forms took shape. It was all Soutine stuff – only different – rough, bloody and raw. I was very pleased with it and promised myself a sabbatical in Praha. There I would see the actual Child of Prague and there I would sit in cellar bars and remember the Bundoran sands and the plaster copy buried upright and radiant.

There is a simultaneous sense of neatness and freedom about my life when the work starts. The urgency is gone, the regular frustration and the self-doubt is suddenly cleared by confident brushwork and the solid, powerful image. I go at it hard and then I go for long, long walks through fields and streets. It is a feeling rarely achieved and even harder to cling too. In this mood even the cockroaches can't get me. But then, two days later, everything took another left turn. A knock at the door.

I had slept in the studio the night before after a long session's painting and, in my morning exhaustion, I dreamt both the knock and the visitor. The knocking continued and the dream of the mysterious visitor at the door was blasted away by the sudden cold and the heartbeat and the realisation and the panic and the rush to the actual door itself. I wondered who it could be and in my delirium I imagined the grandmother, The Cockroach, the Golem, the Child of Prague, the cops . . . I opened the door about as wide as my eyes could manage.

She looked like Ingrid Bergman.

Hi, I'm Billie Maguire.

It was some young girl. No notion who she was.

Yes, can I help you?

May I come in?

Well, I'm very busy at the moment . . . who are you again?

Billie Maguire, I work for Firecracker Films.

Look, I'm not making any documentary for anybody.

Just let me speak with you a moment!

No! I'm sorry!

I was too tired for this but she was alert and persistent.

I'd really love to see your studio, said Billie Maguire with a smile, and there's something good in the paper I wanted to show you.

I was genuinely too tired to argue. I surrendered.

All right! I mumbled angrily, but you'll have to excuse the place . . . it's a bit of a tip.

That was a bad mistake. I'm not in control of my own head in the mornings and her brightness and eager looks were immediately dangerously attractive and stirring. She took everything in, gazing at every piece of canvas, every offcut of board and every strip of paper.

Ah, this is great! she said, scanning the walls.

Yes, well . . . what's in the paper that's so important?

Just this, she shrugged:

DNA TESTS ON ST OLIVER PLUNKETT

She raised her eyebrows in an all-knowing, all-questioning way and I for some reason offered her coffee.

Is it real coffee? she asked.

I shook my head.

In that case I'll skip it thanks.

DNA tests were being carried out on the head of Saint Oliver Plunkett. According to reports in

Technology Ireland samples were being taken from his alleged head which was preserved in Drogheda, and tests were being performed at the University of Southern Florida. The DNA would then be matched with a DNA fingerprint from a living descendant of the martyred Archbishop Plunkett. Monsignor Seamus Moloney said that there was no question but that the head was real and that the tests were being carried out to enhance the visitor's experience.

What do you make of all that? asked Billie Maguire.

It's all phoney, I replied rather predictably.

Have you ever seen the head?

No.

Would it really matter if it was real or not?

No.

That's exactly my point. Now what about you and me making a film about you? Just you and me. Whatever you say goes.

No. I don't do showbiz.

I'm serious. It would be done with all due seriousness and respect. No nonsense.

Do you like my work? I asked suspiciously.

I might and I might not.

I'm very sorry, Ms Maguire, but I'm afraid I have no interest in making a film of any kind. I mistrust the media deeply and I think that your boss is a cockroach.

So do I! He has a moustache! she answered eagerly. So may I call here again tomorrow?

I wasn't at myself and so I think I vaguely agreed – as much to get rid of her as anything else. But I made it clear there would be no film for The Cockroach or his fences.

Next day, Billie Maguire showed up again as threatened and she was all business.

Look, she began, I don't like Clive any more than you do but I promise you that he will have nothing to do with this film. Absolutely nothing! You have my word on that.

I tried once more to knock it on the head. I thought of hammers as I said it.

Look, Ms Maguire, I'm sure you're perfectly all right and your intentions are honourable but I'm just not doing it. End of story.

She wouldn't give up –

You see, yesterday, when we were taking about Oliver Plunkett's head?

What about it?

Well, I know that's what you're interested in. What's real and what's not real. I know your work probably better than you do yourself. I have lived in your exhibitions, dwelt in them – I know what you're about and there'll never be a better record of what makes you tick than a film you might make with me. I'm sympathetic! I care about what's in it! I know your work inside out. Even all that sculpture stuff you did years ago – you remember the exhibition in Dublin – the stuff with the lawnmowers and the saws and the hedge clippers wrapped in tinfoil? Do you remember it? It was called *Tools of the Trade*? That was serious stuff! The hammer and everything! Do you remember . . .

One to forget, I interrupted, I was going through a phase.

Naw it was terrific! Anyway, I know what would appeal to you. You and me make this film together but it'll be your film — any way you want. You call the shots.

I decided to test her out —

OK then. Let's, for the sake of argument, say that I call the shots. You interview me and I tell you nothing but lies. Nothing but absolute lies. Not an ounce of truth in the whole thing. The programme will be a complete fabrication but you will never admit that to anyone. It will be our little secret. The end result will be scrutinised as if it is of some importance and yet I will have the pleasure of knowing that everyone from commissioning editor, to Cockroach, to critic, to government quango has been well and truly suckered. And best of it all, true or false, it won't matter a damn.

Billie Maguire smiled —

Perfect! I love it! It'll be a work of art itself! Oh, I can just imagine Clive . . .

Stop calling him Clive! He is The Cockroach!

All right. I can just imagine him slabbering on about it at dinner parties with all the other cockroaches. Oh, it will be a hoot! Do we have a deal?

We have to go to Prague first, I said.

Prague?

I was a student there.

Were you?

What do *you* think?

Brilliant! Is that us agreed then?

Before I knew it I was locked in. It was my own fault.

One other thing, I snapped, no crew. Just you, me and one of those videocam things. It all has to be between you and me. The first sign of any shite and I'm walking.

CITY HOTEL MORAN, NA NORÁNI 15, CZ – 120 00 PRAHA.

Separate rooms and outside it snowed. The minibar was full of small bottles of red drink. The vodka was frozen. Next door, Billie Maguire was getting ready to go out. I had promised her some fine Bohemian food and so we met in reception. I looked ridiculous in monkey cap and shovel gloves and she glowed like a fairy-tale princess who had just fallen off the back of a troika.

It was very cold out, immediately beautiful and the road signs made little sense as we walked along the Vltava and I talked crap about architecture. The buildings along the embankment were sometimes Paris, sometimes Munich and sometimes Petrograd. Masarykovo something. Smetanovo something and then the glorious Charles Bridge –

What a marvellous piece of medieval architecture, I offered nervously.

You sound like The Cockroach! laughed Billie Maguire.

I shot her what you might call a venomous look.

We stood and gazed across the river – the beautiful

black, saint-lined bridge, the wide freezing river and the magnificent clutter of spires and domes all leading up and up to the Hradčany where Havel was president and the cobbled, lanterned streets were held up by cellar bars of Pilsner Urquell, Gambrinus and Purkmistr.

But before the beer and gaslight – the necessary hagiography as we walk, all of a sudden arm in arm on to the bridge – Jesus, Saint Damian and Saint Cosmas dressed as doctors, Saint Wenceslas, Saint Vitus and the lion who ate him, Saint John of Matha, Saint Felix of Valois and Saint Ivan, Saint Philip Benizi – the man who refused to be pope – in marble, Saint Adalbert, Saint Cajetan, Saint Lutgard having her vision, Saint Augustine, Saint Nicholas of Tolentino, Saint Jude of the hopeless cases, Saint Procopius the Bohemian hermit, Saint Anthony of Padua, the hammer of the heretics, Saint Francis of Assisi, Saint John of Nepomuk who was chucked over the bridge, Saint Ludmilla, the baby Saint Wenceslas, Saint Francis Borgia, Saint Norbert, Saint Sigismund, Saint Wenceslas again, John the Baptist, Saint Christopher, Saint Cyril, Saint Methodius, Saint Francis Xavier, Jesus, Mary and Joseph, Saint Anne, Saint Dominic, Saint Thomas Aquinas, Saint Barbara, the Patron Saint of Miners, Saint Margaret, Saint Elizabeth, another Madonna, Saint Bernard and Saint Ivo, Patron Saint of Lawyers who gets free drink from law students when they've done their finals. Pilsner Urquell, Gambrinus and Purkmistr.

Billie Maguire and myself ate Prague ham and bramborová and were soon as full as forty badgers on neat frozen vodka and sweet black beer. From a framed picture on the wall Václav Havel and Boris Yeltsin toasted our new relationship. On the way back to the hotel, under the statue of Saint Jude, I nervously stabbed her cheek with a kiss and I talked an awful lot of balls. Billie Maguire didn't seem to mind.

THE KING

Titanium white. Flake white. Zinc white.

The first thing I heard was –

Sir, you ever eat squirrel?

And with that simple and yet extraordinary interrogation, The King entered the room with an almighty shrug. He was not as I remembered him and I answered his question politely but in the negative.

Sir, he said quietly, you really oughtta try fried squirrel in butter.

Yes, indeed I must, I agreed. Have you ever attempted fried eel from Toombe? Nice with wheaten bread and stout.

No, sir, I haven't.

Pike perhaps? Or grilled perch from Big Paris Island?

No, sir. I really don't like fish. Can't stand the smell. You ever eaten possum?

I'm afraid not, I answered with some sorrow.

Is a whale a fish?

No. I believe it is a mammal.

Is a possum a mammal?

Yes, I believe it is.

Well, sir, I sure have eaten some of those critters.

Possum, rabbits, squirrels, hogs . . . you ever eat sweet potatoes?

Oh yes, I'm very fond of spuds. I always feel a meal is not a meal without spuds.

You like hot dogs with kraut?

I probably would.

Collared greens?

Oh, certainly. You need your vegetables so you do.

Yes, sir. You sure do.

The above conversation concluded, The King, the Pelvis, Elvis to his mother, adjusted the collar of his grotesque white suit and smiled through the corner of his chubby mouth –

Where you want me to stand, sir?

It was my strangest commission ever. I don't know who was responsible for it but after a series of mysterious phone calls from record company slugbastards, I finally received the summons from the Colonel himself. As he spoke, all I could think of was fried chicken – such are the confusions of popular culture.

Before I knew it I was in Memphis, Tennessee – a limousine sliding through those crotcheted gates and into the inner circle of the Presley court – minders, shirt-tailers, liggers, television producers, hangers-on and other familiar parasites. No point in describing Graceland – you've all seen the pictures and that's just the way it was. I painted him in that large circular room of red and blue lights –

Sir, you like this suit I'm wearing?

79

He raised his arms to reveal the gold lining of the cape that hung about his rhinestone shoulders.

Yes, Mister Presley, I nodded, it's a hoot.

I was worried about the light.

Hell, shrugged Elvis, that don't matter none. I guess you know what I look like already.

The King was right. I could have stayed at home and painted him right out of my head. There were not many people I could have captured just by memory but the image of Presley was one of them. James Joyce was another. His inkwell eyes are easy. I can also dash off the grandmother at the drop of a hat – or Charlie Chaplin and just about anybody with a beard. And so, in almost total gloom, I set about painting the King.

He could only keep still for about a minute at a time and then a sudden shrug would cause an awesome avalanche of material and jewellery and bulk. To make things worse, he kept kicking his feet out in front of him like a shot-putter concentrating before the effort itself. And then there was the constant motion of his forearm, wiping the sweat which dripped in steady meditative beads from his rock 'n' roll chin. Whenever I cautiously asked him to stand still he immediately apologised and, fair play to him, he did his best. He was a very nice man –

Where you from, sir? he asked.

Fermanagh, I replied.

They got squirrels there?

Yes, Mister Presley, they got red squirrels and grey squirrels.

Oh man!

They got Presleys too, you know.

Damn! They got Presleys?

Yes. I believe your ancestors were all Fermanagh men.

Oh man!

Did you never hear of Saint Elvis? Lived on Devenish Island and spent fifty years meditating hard. Sitting on top of a round tower with the point of it inflicting unthinkable pain in the region of his backside?

His butt?

Yes indeed, Mister Presley. He was a very saintly saint. He loved animals and kept a famous herd of deer and three pet hares.

Was his name Presley?

No. He was a Maguire. The first recorded Elvis Presley was hanged for no apparent reason in 1647. Two hundred years later his descendants ended up in America. They were decent people and very musical. All the Presleys were good singers.

Well, sir, I ain't never heard that before. I'm much obliged.

The time passed quickly and he chatted away like a good one. We talked about Robert Johnson and how he went to the crossroads and sold his soul to the Devil and died, barking like a dog, on the sixteenth of August 1938. The King knew his stuff all right and he even sang few bits of songs. He was great company right enough and I recommended a few records by Liam O'Flynn.

The painting worked out great. Only one sitting of course but even so. It was weird, grotesque and very large and I got through a massive amount of white. Flake. Zinc. Titanium. Everything I had. I could tell that Elvis hated the picture but I got paid anyway and before I left, a lovely woman fixed us up two sloppy joes.

I have got my things about me now – my brushes, my palette knife and my rags. Also my guilts and fears and forbears. And now perhaps things will begin to happen as I sketch so lightly with a hard pencil (2H). The image will doubtless soon take shape and the story too as I begin to dab and stroke and scrub and scrape and scratch.

I am a painter and I have admitted from the start that I committed a murder at the age of nine. I accept that it might seem unlikely and I further accept that you might find it all very hard to credit. This was also indicated at the very start when I questioned aloud whether you would believe me or not?

My later life and certain success as a painter is also covered in a rather sketchy way and I elaborate to a certain extent on my views about celebrity, myth and achievement. I hint at my notions on showbusiness and the media and I suggest that I sometimes feel totally surrounded by a fraudulent shower of bastards – e.g., Clive Ratcliff Firecracker Films (The Cockroach) who wants to make a film about me because it will make *him* look good. I later dream that he dies horribly (found in various pieces inside his own filing cabinet). It is also the case that I had earlier threatened to kill him.

I have also dealt in some detail with my family, my childhood, my obsession with saints, holy relics and my Action Man. I have also discussed, to a limited degree, my interest in burying things – the Child of Prague, my legs, whales, seashells, hubcaps and so on.

Some reference is also made to pre-pubescent gang warfare and an inexplicable activity called Scouting. Other than that, much remains a mystery – notably how will I get through secondary school, girls, peer pressure, discos, teenage confusion, mushrooms, art college and notoriety and yet remain in possession of my tenebrous secret?

And what of the Child of Prague headless on the sill? And the fifty-three-foot whale decomposing beneath the myriad grains of damp Donegal sand? And can I ever really go back to caress her whitening bones?

And what of the grandmother – a formidable woman blessed with a deep faith in all things incredible and a great affection for her murderous grandson? How else would I have, for so long, escaped detection and imprisonment? The grandmother is guardian of all, like the big man in Rome with all the terrible secrets locked up in the drawer of his bedside locker.

And how did the grandmother know my secret in the first place? Had she been told in a dream? A visitation? Perhaps during some revelatory apparition on a gable wall? Certainly it wasn't me who told her. Was it a whispered voice? An anonymous tip-off? A tout? A supergrass? Perhaps it was, as she had mentioned, one of the mongrel dogs in the street? Bonzo Brady or Brandy King? Other times I wondered if perhaps the grandmother had made the whole thing up herself and maybe I had never killed anyone at all? Perhaps I had never even been to Bundoran in my puff? Maybe the whole episode was only alive in my young mind as a result of the grandmother's untapped powers of suggestion? It was a possibility too that one of the buckteeth cousins had invented the whole tale just to get me in trouble with the grandmother who so obviously favoured me above each and every one of them? Wouldn't put it past them either, the wee bastards.

Occasionally I would dwell on these as relieving possibilities but then, in inevitable and renewed horror, I had to confront the reality that I had in fact hammered the fossil collector upon the skull with his own geological hammer. After all, I could remember the whole episode in such vivid and shivering detail that I must surely have done it. I could recall every moment of it – the P. M. on the handle, the monkey cap, the crack, the tumble, the splash, the creamy ambulance, the Child of Prague, the grandmother's family gather-up, the oath, the fear, the thumping heart and the cavernous stomach. I had done it all right. It had happened. And one day it all would come out – in dribs and dribs and ominous drabs.

THE CARDBOARD BOX

I sat with Billie Maguire over by the Novotńy Footbridge and the day was warm. Across the calm Vltava, the Hradčany stood in all its fairy-tale glory and Billie Maguire began to roll. The videocam was a masterstroke – just the two of us and an overhanging willow dipping in and out of shot.

I studied here, I began, long before it was popular or profitable. There were very few Irish here – a fair gathering of Americans but other than that it was all Czech and East German. Those were the Cold War days and on more than one occasion I was taken for a spy.

Really? gasped Billie, a spy?

Oh yeah! I lied, regular as clockwork, oh, it was hairy enough at the time.

And so began the bullshit. The documentary without an ounce of truth in it. I had taken notes from a guidebook so as to be convincing with my mispronounced placenames. Stories were dropped about Saint Vitus and John Nepomuk and I couldn't help feeling rather impressive and yet only slightly bogus –

Saint Vitus, I blathered, had exorcised the son of the Emperor Diocletian and was duly appointed the

Patron Saint of epilepsy and of Sydenham's chorea. And then there was John Nepomuk whose statue is the only one in bronze upon the Charles Bridge. You will notice that he is forever surrounded by prayerful and tactile devotees. On the base of his statue there is a relief also in bronze depicting his death. It has been touched and rubbed with so much fervour that the figure of the saint now glows like gold – ah yes – John Nepomuk, hurled off the bridge to his death only to reappear there in 1683 – thus putting manners on non-believers.

Interesting, breathed Billie Maguire, and what was it that attracted you to Prague in the first place?

Oh, I should say that were two things really. One was Good King Wenceslas and the other was, of course, the Child of Prague. To take the Good King first – Wenceslas or Václav was born in 907 and wait 'til you hear this for a family background. The grand-mother was called Ludmilla and she was a Christian. The mother was called Dragomira and she was a pagan and, because of the way things were, the grand-mother was appointed regent when Václav inherited his title at the age of only thirteen. Dragomira took the hump and murdered the granny.

Murdered the granny?

Mmmmh. Murdered the granny. Yes indeed. Murdered the granny. Eventually, Václav became the Duke and decided he would encourage Christianity in his land. He took a vow of celibacy and welcomed German missionaries. Of course, the local Christians took the hump over this and they set about winding up the younger brother Boleslav the Cruel. In September 929, he stabbed and killed Václav. Or Wenceslas as you know him better.

What about the Feast of Stephen then? asked Billie Maguire on the minute.

Feast of Stephen my arse! I responded, not a word about it. Good King Wenceslas was only a duke and he last looked out in September.

Where did you study? continued Billie with a tilt of the camera.

Oh at the university here (I didn't know the name of it). Five good years and perhaps a period when some of my best work was done. I completed a terrific series of paintings on the subject of the golem. You know, Rabbi Loew's clay robot over in the Jewish quarter. I'll talk more on this later because it is very important. And Meyrink who wrote the book – another rare Prague gentleman into the whole Kabbalah thing, as indeed I was myself for a period.

Kabbalah?

Oh yes, Doctor Dee, the whole bit. Meyrink wrote a book about Dee because he was yet another alchemist to walk these cobbled streets. And isn't painting a form of alchemy in itself? The golem. The Action Man. Frankenstein. I made some interesting paintings in those days. It was my Promethean phase. I even built a huge golem out of coat-hangers and newspaper and then late one night I chucked it over the Charles Bridge. It floated great.

Billie lowered the camera from her face and asked –

Can I just ask you, off-camera, are you making this up as you go along?

Yes, I said.

This ramass went on for about fifteen minutes until Billie suddenly announced,

That's a rap for today! Record and print.

I was happy with the morning's work and after wandering the Mala Strana all afternoon, we eventually ended up in the Church of Saint Nicholas. This saint formerly known as Santy Claus was yet another object of belief and disbelief throughout my questioning life. First duped into belief, I was then tipped off into disbelief by the granny. And then suddenly the light bulb of the obvious as I noticed that there were at least three Santa Clauses in my hometown alone. There's no such thing as Santy Claus I finally admitted and the absence was massive.

Do you believe in Santy? I asked Billie Maguire on the slope of Nerudova.

Indeed I do, she replied.

Well, in that case, Billie Maguire, do you believe in God?

Billie Maguire stopped and stared me right in the face.

Ask me an easy one, she said.

Clearly uncomfortable and distant, Billie said she needed an early night and we parted. I headed for a cellar bar beside the US Embassy where Shirley Temple was probably remembering the old days on the Good Ship Lollipop.

★   ★   ★

Nine o'clock call.

INTERIOR. CHURCH.

Panna Maria Vítězná. Karmelitská. Prague. Gloomy but for candle and strip light. Close-up on face of Child of Prague in its kitsch display case. Pull back to reveal the display in its entirety and back of head gazing up. Turn and speak to camera. Medium close-up.

This is the Church of the Barefooted Carmelites in Prague – the Czech Republic – the former Czechoslovakia. This little man behind me in this sparkling fishtank is the Infant of Prague – the real one – the actual one. Not a copy. Not a reproduction like the one that stood guard on the windowsill of my childhood bedroom. Not one of the many that you might find for sale in a religious goods store in Bundoran. Certainly not the same one that I shoplifted from such a shop when I was about nine. This one behind me is the real thing. The Bambino. The Infant. The Child of Prague.

This little man is the reason I came here to study for my chosen path as a painter. Not a very good reason perhaps. But it was here that I found myself as an artist. It was here in Prague that I first discovered what it was I wanted to paint – and perhaps for the first time discovered who I was.

Cut! said Billie Maguire triumphantly as she ushered me outside again. Brilliant! You're a one-take wonder.

It was raining hard outside and I was beginning to enjoy the wickedness of the total lie.

Such shite! I laughed.

Precisely! Billie laughed back.

We were at it again almost immediately. I walked down the steps and along the street and Billie walked backwards in front of me like a soldier with me in her sights.

Now, tell me more about your early days. Remember to look directly into the camera and it's OK to smile.

I composed myself again and began to reel off the biggest load of spoofery ever spoken by a person not normally employed in television. I talked about wild student days in Prague, a tough upbringing back home, a drink problem, a brief spell studying for the priesthood, a trial with Everton, living as a down-and-out in Brussels and my various jobs in abbatoirs, hospitals, the post office and the vineyards of Bordeaux. It all sounded reasonably plausible and Billie Maguire seemed delighted with my ability to do what she referred to as PTCs or Pieces to Camera. No big deal I thought – all it seemed to require was a certain amount of fraudulence and self-love. Wee buns.

We congratulated ourselves heartily that night and enjoyed, once more, various goulash-type dishes and lashings of frozen vodka. There was another almost snog scenario but again it failed to materialise when Billie Maguire's expression changed and she too became frozen. I even thought for one deflating moment that she might boke.

Next morning she was nowhere to be found. I

waited around the lobby for most of the morning but still no sign. Eventually I gave up and wandered the streets – stopping for a string quartet playing Mozart and Dvořák in the Betlemské náměstí and finally climbing up to the Loreto where the bells rang out 'We Greet Thee A Thousand Times'.

And here, more hagiography. Saint Wilgefortis had taken a vow of celibacy but was being forced to marry. She was very unhappy and wait 'til you hear this one! She grew a beard, the wedding was called off and she was crucified.

And then the Santa Casa. Mary's house in Nazareth lifted lock, stock and barrel by removal men angels and dropped off first in Dalmatia and then in Loreto. This house in Prague is a copy of the house in Loreto. The flit was occasioned by the Turks.

And then it became clear that maybe Billie had flitted too. She had disappeared completely. Vanished for a day and a night but then returned all of a sudden flustered and out of breath as if nothing had happened. She had a cardboard box with her and immediately I sensed some disaster. I could feel it gurgling in my water as she placed the box on the bed and stood well back as if it were a bomb.

Go on! she beamed. Open it, it's for you!

I felt that something had slipped beyond my control and that I was at the mercy of something very bad for me indeed. And I was right. I opened the box and realised immediately what she had done. It was the Child of Prague! She had swiped the Child of Prague! Broken into the Panna Maria Vítězná in the middle of the night and stolen the Bambino! The actual Child of Prague! The real one! And there it was in a cardboard box on the edge of my bed!

Billie Maguire smiled away, all pleased with herself, and said that she would go home by rail with the Child of Prague and that there would be no problem. She would meet me in a week.

But Billie! You can't just steal the Child of Prague! They'll be searching the country for it!

Ah! said Billie with a smug smile, they don't even know it's missing! I replaced it!

With what? One from Bundoran?

No. Not exactly.

With what then?

For a moment Billie Maguire's eyes flashed entirely full of evil.

With an Action Man! The one in the glass case right now is an Action Man – and nobody will know until the next time they change his clothes. Didn't you paint an Action Man once all dressed up as the Child of Prague?

When I was done screaming I sat on the floor with my head in my hands. Billie Maguire fixed her hair at the dressing-table and the head of the Child of Prague peeped out of his cardboard box on the bed. In the Panna Maria Vítězná, pilgrims were gazing in adoration at a former French Foreign legionnaire all dressed up to the nines in clothes provided in 1894 by a village outside Shanghai. A village called Tou-se-we.

THE CURE

On the plane out of Prague, all jittery and holding my breath, I sketched in biro a reasonable likeness of Billie Maguire on the back of a boke bag. She was murder all right. You go on ahead, she said. She would follow overland by train and get the boat from Le Havre to Rosslare. How in hell's blazes, I wondered, would she ever manage to do that with the Child of Prague in her suitcase? Surely somewhere along the line she would be stopped and lifted? Surely the Czechs would be after her – not to mention Interpol, the customs, An Garda Síochana, the Royal Ulster Constabulary, the Catholic Boy Scouts of Ireland, the Legion of Mary, Opus Dei and the entire Carmelite Order?

I passed the following days in sweat and panic, drinking red wine by the half-pint glass – just watching and wondering and waiting for the knock. There was no word at all for three days until suddenly, out of the blue, the granny was on the phone. The granny on the phone! I was astonished. Up until that very moment I had believed with all my heart and soul that she had been stubbornly incapable of operating one – catchpennies she called them –

And the whole country knowin' your business!

She told me that a cuttie had arrived at the front door, announced herself as a friend of mine and had deposited with her a cardboard box containing 'the loveliest wee Child of Prague you ever laid eyes on'. And what's more, the pain in the granny's back had completely gone.

Within minutes I was on the motorway, the local news of flower-arranging in church halls already beginning to fade from the radio as I hurtled west towards Ballygawley, Augher, Clogher, Fivemiletown and over the bump and into Fermanagh twinned with Bielefeld. What was Billie Maguire up to? First to steal the Child of Prague from under the red shiny noses of the Prague Carmelites, then to dash across Europe with the little man in a cardboard box and then to leave the said icon in the possession of the pious granny? I felt hot, weak, sweaty and nervous and the flashing whinbushes were beginning to induce a very bad pain in the head.

And so to the granny's house in the corner of the estate in the corner of the glen. The sight that greeted my two eyes simultaneously was an extraordinary one. A hundred or so people were scattered about, standing smoking butts in the front garden, sinking into the privet hedge or leaning lazily against the gable wall. The front door was open and a steady procession of men, women and children were entering the hall with great gravitas. It was like a wake house and sure enough the curtains were pulled in every blind window. For a brief moment I considered that the ancient grandmother might be dead, but no sooner had the panic of that thought gathered in my belly, than out she galloped through the front door, aprons and wisps of hair flying in all directions – her stoop clearly vanished.

Come on! Come on! she scolded, what kept you at all! Out gallivantin' I suppose!

What's goin' on here, Granny?

C'mon, son! The back is cured!

I thought briefly of bacon but suddenly the jittery meaning of it all revealed itself. All these people were here for a cure! This was Ballinspittle, Knock, Fatima, Lourdes, moving statues and tearful Madonnas. The granny was at the heart of a cult and she was up to high doh –

Come on, son, quick to you see! Up the stairs quick!

And she gripped me hard by the arm and dragged me through the crowds who parted like the Red Sea before her. It was like a wake house right enough – lines of grave figures standing awkwardly and all angles with cups of tea and not knowing for the life of them what to say to anybody. And then the odd laugh like a virus.

The crowds intensified at the back bedroom and the mumble gradually died to a heavy silence within. Again, the people parted and serious faces turned to politely scrutinise myself and the granny. Looking straight ahead all I could see was the former card table with lit candles of differing heights at each corner and the very Child of Prague itself standing solid and triangular in permanent benediction.

All around people knelt and prayed very hard. The more devout among them even seemed to direct some of their piety towards the granny and she didn't seem to mind. After all, her bad back had been miraculously cured by the miraculous little man from Prague who had miraculously appeared in a cardboard box.

This was a real mess. The granny's house was now a shrine and there were television crews arriving outside – a clatter of English reporters from the local BBC and, wouldn't you know it, even that bastard Cockroach was making some alleged documentary – apparently he had always been interested in the Child of Prague and had been meaning for years to do a documentary about folk superstition blah blah blah.

And in the local paper:

LOCAL ARTIST'S GRANNY IS LIVING SAINT!
CROWDS FLOCK TO FAMOUS LOCAL PAINTER'S GRANNY
CHILD OF CORNAGRADE CURES LOCAL INSURANCE MAN

But here's the real story. Billie Maguire steals the actual Child of Prague, replaces it with a dressed-up Action Man and heads across Europe, arriving finally at the granny's house. She deposits with the granny a cardboard box containing the little man and once again vanishes. The granny gets curious, recognises the statue as a Child of Prague (but not as *the* Child of Prague) and duly places him on the card table. Her back is immediately cured, her stoop straightens out and she tells the neighbours. Between them they decide that it must be a miracle and soon the house is full of people with bad backs, ingrown toenails, nerves, headaches, fallen arches, etc, etc. Bedlam. Hysteria. Cautious clerics. Television crews. Newspaper men. Student priests.

Soon it is discovered that the famous artist (me) was in Prague two weeks previous and, what's more, on the very night that the real Child of Prague was swiped from the church. I am maliciously linked with an alleged theft of the Bambino even though no such theft is confirmed. A snap of me standing in front of the Child of Prague is published in the paper. Billie Maguire is nowhere to be seen.

Mysterious people from various embassies start questioning the granny. She says nothing in case she gets lifted and is, in any case, overcome by her own newly confirmed and unassailable saintliness. I get questioned also. A bewildered detective tells me that the Czechs know damn well what has happened but that it would be too great an embarrassment for them to take any formal steps. They would never, reasons the detective, admit that for the past two weeks pilgrims had been praying to an Action Man.

He clearly just wants to go home as he is, as he puts it, 'of the other persuasion' and knows nothing of statues or orders of nuns. Even so, he warns me that they'll be watching me like a hawk.

After a fortnight of chaos, bus trips and numerous alleged cures the granny somewhat reluctantly donates the Child of Prague (now known as the Child of Cornagrade) to the local church where it is given some prominence in a side altar. She has her photograph taken for posterity – a holy and serene one – and she regularly fantasises that the Pope will make a visit soon, hold her by the shoulders and declare her a saint. She imagines his red shoes padding softly up the red lino stairs and she giggles out loud.

THE PRESIDENT

It was a dark, wet and wintry evening when the grandmother clung tighter than ever to my bony arm and we angled ourselves into the downpour and ascended the glistening black avenue to a new and ominous place called Saint Basil's Grammar School.

I had passed the thing called 'the qually' and was thereby entitled to squeeze behind a desk in this tunnelled and corridored place – shadowy like Hades and slippery underfoot with fearsome portraits of bishops constantly developing out of black nooks.

Saint Basil's teetered on a craggy outcrop and I thought at once of Transylvania. We should by rights have arrived by caleche – four black horses snorting two abreast and driven by a cowering manservant with a hump. But we tramped up on foot and the only weird welcome we got was from the school crest – its motto in a hairline fracture Latin mosaic – *jiggere, pokere* something – some kind of mumbo-jumbo embedded in ancient eggshells or the flaky bones of boys.

The polished floor might have been a shiny, rinky kind of Hollywood slide for Gene Kelly to glide across and fall on his knees and keep on moving frictionless all thighs and teeth. But it was not.

This was not Hollywood. This was stale, dark and gloomy with all the sacred furniture of the Catholic boys' grammar school. It was sinister as hell and the grandmother had me by the elbow – all right angles and nervous.

Now you behave yourself in front of this man! Do you hear me!

The president's room, when we found it, was dark and full of books – not real books with spines untidy and various, but the sorts of books that never get opened – canon law, encyclopaedia-type books – all leather with faded gilt lettering, regimented and dull. The headmaster himself seemed civil enough and he smoked a Sherlock pipe and wrestled constantly with plug tobacco and a penknife not up to the job. He was, the grandmother had professed, a real brainbox. His kind and soft demeanour seemed immediately out of place.

From amid his clouds of smoke, he told me that I would be expected to study for three hours a night and I thought that this was both horrific and unlikely. Some friggin' chance, Father, I thought to myself – three hours of homework would leave little room for fossil-gathering, fish-catching, football-kicking and cuckoo-calling. It appeared that this place had very strange notions about what was important and that my rich and varied life would be of no real consequence in this new and strange world.

He's a living saint, Father, the grandmother explained, a living saint . . .

I'm sure he is indeed a good boy, ma'am. But

canonisation is, alas, a long way away off for all of us . . . but we shall see. Everyone will be treated fairly in this school. Three hours' study every night and an adherence to school rules. Have you any questions?

I had no questions. The grandmother had only the one –

Father, is there still such a thing as Limbo?

She was always on about Limbo. She said it was some place near Heaven and that nobody seemed too sure whether it existed or not these days. I knew nothing about it either but I had seen a Limbo dancer once. His name was King Bob and he was the star attraction in the circus over by Modern Tyre Service. It was me who saw his name on the poster – King Bob, World Champion Limbo Dancer – and it was me who rounded up a small posse to go to the show after school.

He was baldy black man in his bare feet and he could lean backwards until the back of his head nearly touched the ground. He wore a glittery-gold waistcoat and a bright-red nappy and when they set fire to the bar he passed no remarks and just shimmied under it with a big smile on his face. We thought he was great and we clapped and whooped.

In the car park afterwards we found his caravan and he looked very annoyed. His toenails looked like the shells of snails.

What do you want? he asked impatiently.

We asked him for his autograph and then wandered off confused. When we saw the baggy clowns having a smoke we asked for their autographs too.

They wrote their short one-word names and asked us if we had been to the circus. Then a woman with a bony face and a hooky nose appeared and snapped all the bits of paper from us and tore them up into little bits and ordered us to go home. She must have been in charge of King Bob and the clowns and the sad, scattered bits of paper and pencil scrawls lay in the mud like a sad mosaic, the school crest or one of the patterns we made in art.

But this was a different kind of Limbo altogether and the grandmother quizzed the priest about it and I asked if I could wait outside.

The corridors were eerie and echoey. In the distance, I thought I could hear the speedy, tipped brogues of another invisible priest and so I hushed along in the opposite direction and found myself in sudden and deeper darkness, overcome by a nightmare fear. I was trapped in the late-night silent tunnels of a hospital, a prison, a mental hospital from some Victorian book, the workhouse, a forest full of eyes.

I clung to the wall and knocked some picture crooked. In the space of an empty second I imagined its smash carrying around the caverns and the sleepy doors opening one at a time – old bony priests emerging from their sepulchres – half awake and half alive. I ran hard on my tiptoes back to the room which contained the grandmother and the kindly president and I rapped the door. The president's voice said –

Enter!

I stepped inside holding on to the doorknob with both hands and spinning awkwardly around the door's flaky length. The president stood up. The grandmother stood up.

Thank you, Father, she said.

And then, looking me in the two eyes, the priest said –

We'll be seeing you very soon.

The grandmother gripped me once again by the elbow and we shuffled out into the dark.

What were you talking about, Granny? I asked as soon as we got out into the wind.

Limbo, she whispered . . .

What did he say?

Talking through his hat, son, talking through his hat.

We ran in short, stunted steps down the avenue, the wind and rain blowing us over on to the muck of the grass verge. It was pitch black and you couldn't see your finger.

I don't like that place, I said.

Ah well, son, you go there and get yourself a good education. It'll stand to you. They can't take it off you. Just pass no remarks on anything the clergy tell you. Do you hear me talking to you. Pass no remarks on them. Half of them aren't that bright.

The next morning we hitched it to the Well of the Holy Women and went through the usual rigmarole with the stones.

And in the paper:

It's a person called Kamm. It says he's a prophet. He says Hale-Bopp is going to hit the sun. Earthquakes, tidal waves and the whole lot. He says it's God sending us messages. He says the Pope will leave Rome and there will be a third world war. We must repent.

LIFTED

Bless me, constables, for I have sinned. It has been twenty long years since my last confession. I wish to spill the beans. I wish to make a statement.

That said, the two cops looked confused and told me to keep quiet. But I persisted.

I wish, I declared, to get it off my chest! Wipe the slate clean!

Once again, and in a strange harmony, they ordered me to shut up. They told me that they would ask the questions and that I would answer them and that this simple procedure would make everything as painless as possible. I nodded and smiled –

I wish, I said, to sing like canary!

At last I had finally been lifted. After years of the grandmotherly warnings, the nightmares and the premonitions, it had actually happened. Lifted! I was in custody!

But even so, this was not for any sort of questioning about the senseless murder of a palaeontologist with a hammer in the early seventies, this was to help the police with their inquiries into the alleged theft of the Child of Prague from under the runny noses of the Carmelites. I was nervous but somehow relieved that something inevitable was finally happening.

The two cops were bald as coots – one of them had a shiny head and the other had a matt one. A right pair of culchie bastards, I would have thought and, between the two of them, they had four hairy hands. The four famous hairy hands, the ten famous hairy fingers of Tweedledum and Tweedledee.

They leant over me in an a strangely intimate huddle and seemed to roll like Spacehoppers – or those other inflatable things that you could punch but would never fall over. They were roundy men but somehow jagged about the eyes – eyes which each seemed to know were his most effective weapons. Sharp eyes, mad eyes, crabbed eyes.

We were quite the tableau. The two interrogators, the light bulb, the darkness, the minuscule suspect – all of us glowing in the lamplight like some fine Caravaggio in bold and threatening chiaroscuro. I thought of movies and the television. Good cop. Bad cop. Cigarettes. The ties coming off. I tried again.

Bless me, constables, for I have sinned. I confess to Almighty God and to you, Tweedledum and Tweedledee, and all my brothers and sisters that although I am a virtual only child, I did it. I killed him. Stone dead. As a doornail. I was only nine and I hit him with a hammer. Sack of spuds. I know that makes me below the age of criminal responsibility but I'm not sure about the law in the Free State. Maybe there's some kind of statute of limitations too? And what about double jeopardy? What's all that about? I don't know what way any of that works but I'm sure that you two fat bastards would be fit to tell me. He was a palaeontologist. Fossils. Ammonites. The Loch Ness Monster. Ichthyosaurs. Icarus. Led Zeppelin. Saint Hilda and headless serpents. They ought to lock me up and throw away the key. I'm a bad egg, boys, and no mistake. I crossed the line, gentlemen. The Maginot. The one that Johnny Cash walks. The thin line, boys. So much for Joseph of Cupertino and the rest of them. Officers, sergeants, detectives, generals, admirals, emperors – whatever yous are – I want to make a statement.

Tweedledum and Tweedledee looked at each other and so simultaneously did they reach the same sudden level of indignation that you might have thought they were the same person – the two baldy heads sprouting from the same spherical source –

Listen here, son, said Tweedledee, his hairy hands curled up into fists, you won't act the playboy in here. I don't give two fucks what you did when you were nine. I'm here to tell you that we know what you were at in the former Eastern Bloc and we're fuckin' on to you. So none of your fancy fuckin' poeticals in here!

Did yis not hear what I said?

I'm warning you! shouted Tweedledee right into my face. I'll put fuckin' manners on you, boy!

And so fuckin' well will I, added Tweedledum with equal venom.

Tweedledee suddenly slapped the desk –

Lookit, I don't know anything about statues, nuns or Czechoslovakia and I don't give a fuck. You stole that statue, you're one fuckin' lucky man because the

Czechs don't want a fuss. I'm just telling you that if I had my fuckin' way I'd knock seven shades of shite out of you. So you just remember that we're watching you and if you so much as think about stealing anything in this jurisdiction, you'll be one sorry fuckin' man.

I hope, I said, yous didn't use language like that the day yous passed out.

At this point I think I was hit. All I remember is coming round with a sore jaw. I immediately resumed.

I want to make a statement! There is an old black and white called *A Reckless Moment* and although I have never seen it myself, I think it might have some bearing on my own case. It stars James Mason and Joan Bennett and she wears horn-rimmed spectacles. James Mason was in *Lolita* too but this is a different one. Joan Bennett is in this one and her daughter Beatrice hits a man over the head with a torch. Then she runs away and goes to bed totally unaware that the man later falls in the sea and is found dead the next morning by the mother who then sets about covering up the whole thing. Perhaps if they were to make a movie about the Bundoran incident, they might hire herself to play the granny. I'd say she'd be very dear though.

The film is set in Balboa, California, and I was there myself one time in the company of another painter and we were informed that John Wayne had lived in the vicinity. The painter had never heard tell of John Wayne.

I paint myself you know. Horses. Coots. Whales. That's what I do for a living. I could do you two fat bastards at the drop of a hat. So what do you make of that? The girl used a torch but I used a hammer. I suppose it would be a heavy enough yoke with them big batteries it it.

Tweedledum lit a cigarette and breathed deeply through his nostrils. Tweedledee's head began to twitch violently as he said more bad words. There was a long silence as we looked at each other. They clearly didn't know what to do.

Look, I shouted, I'm going to make a confession if I have to beat it into you!

After that they left me there alone and I began to talk to my old friend the wall –

Right, wall, here goes. The whole story. *Confessio.* I said bad words, I told lies and I had bad thoughts but to be honest I don't really think that's much of a sin anyway. What else did I do? Oh yes I threw stones at a bird, I kicked the coal shade, I didn't do what the granny told me and I coveted the neighbour's Action Man because it had the gripping hands and mine couldn't hold a note. I swallowed the chewing gum one time and I talked during Mass and I stole an apple out of the staffroom, bored a hole in it, filled it with salt and put it back. I smoked a pipe in P7 and I killed a fossil collector. Hit him on the head with a hammer. A small hammer. A geological hammer. And don't tell me I'm imagining it. Ask the granny. She'll back me up. I never stole the Child of Prague but I know who did and I won't tell you because

I'm no supergrass. For these and for all my sins I am very sorry.

Ego te absolvo. Ego te absolvo. Ego te absolvo. Ego te absolvo.

But then I realised that I was alone and that Tweedeledum and Tweedledee had gone. I put my forehead down on the desk and finished up the jigsaw without even once looking at the pieces.

And in the paper:

NOBODY'S AFRAID
OF THE BIG BAD WOLF NOW

Turns out that the poor wolf they've been chasing round Fermanagh is no more a lupine than I am myself. And they shot the poor animal in the Knocks and sent its head to Oregon for tests – DNA analysis and the whole bit. Anyway, the wolf was a dog. A bow-wow at the heel of the hunt. After the helicopters and the spotter planes pursuing the unfortunate creature across Brookeborough's estate and tally-ho bejapers and all. Romulus and Remus. Its only mistress is the moon, it says. That terrible and tender tribe. And the Ulster Museum thinking about putting this alleged wolf on display beside the mummy. Just goes to show you that nothing is ever what it is supposed to be – and the dogs in the street know it.

DON'T START ME TALKING

And what of Billie Maguire Maguire Maguire? She who is by all accounts guilty of theft under the terms of the legislation – with the intention of permanently depriving etc., etc. And who knows, maybe even some other assorted crimes under her belt while we're at it? Something to do with heresy perhaps or blasphemy? Guilty too of who knows what as far as the laws of the Czech Republic might be concerned, and God-knows-what-not-all if we are to go by the rules of the former Communist boys. And on top of that there is the canon law that only the priest in the college would know about and maybe even some specific law to do with the Carmelites – the law of the convent – nuns' law. With a Carmelite in one hand and so forth.

Billie Maguire was last heard of dropping me in it the day she dropped the little man from Prague at the granny's house and subsequently disappeared from view – apparently evaporating into the ether and taking the historical Maguire family name with her into the void. Where could she be at all? And whatever could she be at?

At this point, I have to admit, I had no ideas on the matter whatsoever. And the granny was no use to me either being so enamoured with her newly acquired saintliness, her visits to the holy wells and her dreams of a Papal visitor. The whole thing was a puzzle and a conundrum of outrageous proportions You couldn't be up to that, Billie Maguire, I kept repeating with a sigh. Couldn't get out of bed early enough for that one.

Each evening I would lie upon my Jackson Pollock floorboards and speculate. Was she perhaps a secret agent? An undercover policewoman? A plain-clothes nun? A spook? An angel? A tax inspectress? A figment of my imagination? A murderess? A stalker? My long-lost sister perhaps or maybe part of some elaborate practical joke being played upon me by my many soup-taking and fraudulent enemies?

Most of these theories I would discount as the night wore on. Didn't she work for The Cockroach's production company? And hadn't we been in Prague together, engaged in a subversive filmic stunt of a documentary nature, and hadn't we almost kissed on the Charles Bridge beneath the statue of Saint Jude? Hadn't we laughed and joked about what we were doing and all of my spoofing and pieces to camera? Wasn't she beautiful and didn't she have sparkling eyes? Didn't she look like Ingrid Bergman? Didn't she wear a white dress?

Not that I ever fancied Ingrid Bergman – I'm more of a Sophia Loren man myself. And there I was in an Italian reverie full of red wine and sunlight and the beautiful Sophia in one of those movie peasant dresses with her shiny shoulders and her flashing thighs and the little rivulet of sweat saying yahoo! as it rolled gleefully into her cleavage and suddenly a knocking at the door. It was not Sophia Loren. It was not Ingrid Bergman either. It was Billie Maguire with a big face on her and a blue plastic bag full of tins of beer –

Hello, she said.

Hello, yourself, I said back.

Can I come in? she said.

I suppose you might as well, I said.

Have you been drinking? she said sniffing the air in front of me.

Like a fish, I said, stretching out once more on the floorboards and pointing my chin at the ceiling. Billie sat down beside me and opened a can.

Do you know, Billie Maguire Maguire Maguire, that you have caused me some serious bother? Do you know that you have introduced a certain chaos into my life? Do you know that I was lifted and near got jail for stealing the Child of Prague – something, might I remind you, that I had nothing whatsoever to do with? Do you realise that, Billie Billie Billie Ma-guire?

Ah poor you! she sneered, I'm sorry for your trouble!

A wicked smile lit up her eyes and yet somehow mysteriously, that very smile of sorts was never repeated in the region of her lips – both of them remaining stern and uncurled.

See you! It's all me, me, me, isn't it? Me, me, me!

I did not respond too well to that remark. And so I made another grand speech.

You come in here! Into my life! How dare you! I'm supposed to be a painter! And what's more, you force me into making a television programme against my will and, into the bargain, you steal the Child of Prague, turn the grandmother into a living saint and you get me lifted! Do you realise that I'm a marked man? Do you know that spooks are watching every move I make!

And do you know what Billie Maguire said? Do you know what her response was to my red-faced, hot-eared declarations? She called me a big baby!

And so I blubbered and before I knew it, confused being that I am, I was once again talking baloney into the lens of her box Brownie. Don't ask me why I did it! All I'm saying is that before long I was back rambling away into that rolling tape and digging an even bigger hole for myself. A deep, dark hole like Noon's Hole – a hole that years and years ago, Francie Maguire's uncle fell into and never came out of. And so down I tumbled with all the reckless abandon of someone who secretly wants to fall, to be found out, to be exposed to all and sundry. It seemed suddenly compulsive, liberating and insane.

How do you feel at this precise moment? she asked.

I'm not at myself, I replied.

How so? she asked with her eyebrows.

I'm exhausted, tired and frustrated. I get like this when I'm not working.

Do you think artists have a streak of madness?

The ones I know have it certainly. But it's not the same madness that you get in other people. Not like the madness you see in dictators or disc jockeys but it's madness all the same.

Are you mad?

As a cut snake.

Really?

Without a doubt. I can get very wound up sometimes, like when you point that thing at me. I feel like I don't know what. And there are people I dream about all the time in these violent dreams. I'm beating them senseless and they are always people I know. Mind you, it's all clean stuff, though, and nobody gets killed or anything. I just punch them with movie punches like the way Gregory Peck would do it if he were to lose the rag. I just throw one satisfying punch after another and their heads flay from side to side, cheek to cheek, and they crash through tables and doors and walls but they don't ever go down until the very last minute so there's never any need to pull them up by the hair or kick them in the stomach. It's just a series of powerful left hooks and right jabs and uppercuts. I'm a southpaw you see. Have you seen me paint? I lead with the right and all the time I'm hammering these people I'm talking away to them and telling them how much I despise them and everything they represent. It's a recurring dream and certain individuals keep featuring over and over again too. The parasites, the frauds and monsters.

And who are these people?

The Cockroach is one.

Anybody else?

I'm not saying. No way, José. If any of these people were ever to be found dead in a heap I would get the blame, wouldn't I? In each case I'd have a definitive motive.

Are you drunk?

As a skunk. You want to open one of those cans?

And still the camera rolled and I kept talking. I was so full of myself that I sensed that Billie Maguire's eagerness to hear what I was saying was almost sexual – ballocks that I am. And so, I showed off – stupid, attention-seeking, ever-so-easy male that I am. Off I went spouting, spoofing and spilling the hills of beans all over the shop – launching headlong into confession after confession after confession.

But this litany of sin was not one of pipe-smoking or orchard-raiding. This was not the kicking of the coal shade or the Sophia Loren shining shoulders. This was not some venial sin hovering around the bottom of the Top Thirty. This was straight in at number one with the murder of our man the palaeontologist in the Atlantic breeze of beautiful Bundoran. This was hammer horror, going-over-like-a-sack-of-spuds, big, mortal, black-sin-on-your-potato-soul stuff. Bless me, Billie Maguire, for I have sinned . . .

Would you believe me, I began, if I told you that I was only nine years of age when I killed him? Would you believe me if I told you that I killed him stone dead and that the granny was mortified?

Billie Maguire shifted in her seat. I composed myself.

I'm telling you all of this, Billie Maguire, because nobody will believe it anyway. And after all, isn't this film meant to be some kind of creative work? We might as well give it some significance, eh? It would be a bit like that half a cow thing or the sheep in the urine. It would be like putting a real dead person inside a sculpture. Was that Fu Manchu or what? You know that kind of freak show horror stuff? Anyway, your film that was first intended to have no truth in it all, will now contain a horrible truth − not that anyone will believe it. Not even you, Billie Maguire, because you won't believe me either. Nobody ever believes me! Nobody ever believes a fucking word I say!

Billie Maguire breathed deeply and checked her camera. Then with a twist of her neck she signalled that I had her full attention. I continued.

I once killed a man. He was a palaeontologist − that's to say a collector of fossils. It happened on Roguey Rock in a place called Bundoran in the County of Donegal. I was nine years old and I was wandering about the rockpools putting in the day and passing the time among the sea mice and the barnacles. The fossil man was tapping gently and looking at everything very closely. I watched him for ages. He must have been a brainbox.

Anyway, to cut a long story short we got talking, he gave me his hammer and I hit him with it when he wasn't looking. He hit his head off a rock and fell in the sea. His body was found by fishermen. I don't know a thing about him. I don't even know his name. And if the granny knew I was telling you this, she'd have my life.

But the granny was never to find out. The phone call which interrupted my confession was from one of the buckteeth cousins. I was to come home straight away. The granny was dead.

REQUIEM

Our crowd were on one side of the church – the aunts, the uncles and the buckteeth cousins who sat in two grim lines and seemed to be gnawing at the back of the pews in front of them. The moo-moo slaughtering father was sitting bolt upright like he had just emerged from a dream and wasn't quite sure where he was. The absent mother and the absent sister remained precisely that. We were a rum crowd.

The other side of the church appeared reserved for the good people of the parish. A flock of nuns picked at their prayer books and holy civilian women in headscarves moved their lips rapidly and occasionally whispered – all there to publicly pay their respects to the sanctified memory of the saintly grandmother.

Some of my associates – Billie Maguire, a few painters, a bad poet, an ex-girlfriend who had shaved her head and a member of a well-known rock band had attached themselves to the holy women wing. None of them, whatever their regard for me, were prepared to be connected with the two rows of weirdos that constituted my extended family. But I can never think less of them for it. I too would have preferred to have been sitting with the Sisters of Mercy.

Between both sets of mourners stood a roundy priest who seemed in great humour altogether and two slumping altar boys with their bulky trainers showing beneath their soutanes. I remember thinking that the priest seemed to be getting rounder by the minute – inflating into some priestly balloon who might at any minute float off to the rafters like Joseph of Cupertino. That would have been a laugh.

One of the altar boys held a large cross, the other a chasuble, but their minds were on other things – football perhaps or computer games, or the dirigible celebrant about to explode into a million relics of himself.

The Child of Cornagrade – né Prague – had been moved into a position of greater prominence and throughout the service I gazed at the little man and thought about Billie Maguire and Prague and the grandmother and the police and the documentary film and The Cockroach and the moo-moo slaughtering father and the Olive Oyl mother and Boot the unmentionable sister and how I would ever go about painting the grandmother now that she could never sit for me. The poor grandmother – the only one who had ever believed me. The poor grandmother who now lay before us at the altar rails – dead to the world.

The words were said, the holy water was splashed and soon I was putting my arm around the shoulder of a buckteeth cousin, the solid weight of the coffin beginning to press itself on the bone of my shoulder. It was as if I would be pushed through the very tiles of the aisle itself into the muck and the concrete and the sand and the rocks and the clay on which the church was built – the very same tiles I noticed that were on the floor of Blakes of the Hollow only down the street. God, Granny, you're wild heavy, I thought to myself as I pressed my ear to the wood for comfort.

Inside her coffin, the grandmother's ear listened to my whispers – her taut-skinned face seeming to smile, all cosied up in silky pink material. There's no pockets in a shroud, she used to say. You can't take it with you.

Don't forget to dig me up in a hundred years, she whispered, and see if I have been preserved like Saint Bernadette or bog butter.

I will surely, I said.

Don't forget now!

I won't. Haven't I to go back to dig up the whale in Bundoran?

You're terrible, man, she said, you never know what to be at. Who else is carrying this coffin?

I'm afraid it's the buckteeth cousins.

Wee skitters! Are the nuns here?

They are.

Good. Grand lassies them nuns. Am I too heavy for you, son?

You're a ton weight!

Mind you don't hurt yourself.

I'll be OK.

The grandmother was buried on the side of a mountain and everybody said that she had been a living saint. Some people lifted jam jars full of clay from the grave and took them home with them certain sure the mouldy muck would have powerful properties – a cure for the warts or whatever. Everybody shook my hand and said they were sorry for my trouble and I said thank you. Billie Maguire hovered nearby and only approached when The Cockroach appeared from behind a yew and I began to lash at him with the very spade which had been used to plant the grandmother.

He tried to embrace me! And he said that he had always been interested in funerals and had been putting together a proposal for a network strand called 'Funeral Rites in the Province'. And so I reared up like a young King Arthur and drew the perfect spade from the mound of earth, swinging it within inches of his head. I could have cleaved him. I should have cleaved him.

But Billie bloody Maguire stopped me and all the stragglers began to leave at speed, mumbling to themselves and looking at me funny. Well, what did they expect me to do? Ms Maguire escorted her Cockroach boss to safety.

Good man yourself, the grandmother said. Take no nonsense from boys like that. And watch that cuttie too. I'm not so sure about her any more either – she's up to something. Now away home, son, and make yourself a cup of tea.

Right, I'll talk to you soon.

Bye bye, son.

And I walked back to the grandmother's house

in the corner of the estate with the very spade that buried her over my sore shoulder. Her house was quiet. The blinds pulled. The fire unlit. The clocks stopped.

MISTER PICASSO

And in the paper:

It seems they have found their feet in Kerry. The
oldest footprints in Europe and they belong to a
Munster tetrapod from Valentia Island. According
to my friends the palaeontologists, this is the earliest
evidence in Europe of quadruped vertebrates. Members of the public can view casts of the fossil prints
in the Geology Department at University College
Cork or at Valentia Heritage Centre. They'll have to
protect the site from eager visitors and unscrupulous
maniacs with hammers – characters like myself or
that man who went for the Michelangelo's Pietà.
This thing would have been a big lizard. And there's
a photograph of the footprints and do you know what
they're using to give scale? A geological hammer no
less. A similar yoke certainly.

And sometimes she calls me Mister Picasso and asks
me if there's anything good in the paper.
  Anything good in the paper, Mister Picasso? she

will say as she passes by. But she's not really that interested and she never listens much.

And in the paper:

GALLERIES ON ALERT AFTER VOMIT ATTACKS

Art galleries across America are up to high doh after an art student who has already admitted vomiting over two other paintings has threatened to strike again. He boked over *Port du Havre* by Raoul Dufy and something else by Mondrian in the Museum of Modern Art in New York. I know it's New York but even so – our man the puke says that the work is so bourgeois that it makes him throw. I read a book one time about someone boking over a painting in the National Gallery in Dublin but to tell you the truth I didn't believe it. But there you are. Truth is stranger than. But not the same thing as.

And sometimes I imagine her gliding by in her white dress and holding my hand and tousling my hair and saying –

Are you all right there, Mister Picasso? Still at the drawing?

And in the paper:

BOB DYLAN SINGS FOR PONTIFF

I must be imagining things.

Any news, Mister Dylan, enquires the Pope, about the Child of Prague?

I think, says Bob, I know the boy who done it.

I'll fix him good and proper, says the Holy Father.

VOCATION

I do not recall that I ever learnt anything of note while attending Saint Basil's Grammar School for Boyos up on the craggy outcrop beyond. It seems, in fairness, that learning was not the actual function of the place anyway. It all seemed much more to do with the colour of your trousers, what side of the corridor you walked on, how long your hair was and an equally strict dogma about not being allowed to hang around the radiators when you arrived in soaked to the skin at half past eight on a pitch-black morning.

The teachers didn't seem to actually know very much either and, any of them that did, eventually left to become insurance men, golfers and ballad singers. They knew nothing much about football or what was the capital of Bolivia or what was the difference between a house martin and a swallow and a swift and they had no hobbies at all apart from cards. They were called lay teachers – civilians who were allowed to wear their own moustaches as long as they never slagged the church or said a bad word.

The priestie boys themselves had to wear the dandruffy black uniforms and only the trendy pain-in-the-arse ones ever grew moustaches. These groover clerics were supposed to be charismatics, whatever that was, and they tried to get in with us by talking about John Denver even though we hated John Denver and only liked Horslips and the Undertones. Charismatics were the acoustic guitar wing of the Roman Catholic Church and I didn't like the look of them.

I remember one time when one of the holy strummers hauled me out of the tuck-shop queue and hit me a deadly slap in the face. It was stinging and sore but I wasn't allowed to slap him back because I would be expelled if I did. I couldn't even defend myself a wee bit because I would be expelled for raising my arm. And so it was an unfair fight and I had to stand there looking at his stupid trendy glasses and say nothing even though it was a case of mistaken identity and a gross miscarriage of justice. If I ever meet him on a dark night he'll be one sorry man. I am the hammer of the heretics! Revenge for Skibbereen! Garotted with a guitar string and buried in bits beneath the handball alley.

Some of the priests were nice enough though and would never do you a bad turn at all. These were the genuine holy joes who were always praying before school started – praying for their poor mothers and their poor fathers and their poor grandmothers and the poor lover they had to leave behind in their distant teens and who was now married to a big Monaghan farmer who took a strap to her seven children whenever they were bold. I knew they would rather have gone fishing or maybe just listen to music than spend the whole grey day calling out the roll and checking the spellings. They would rather have been anywhere else – and those were the ones I liked.

And so, I ask myself often, what did I learn in that place and those seven long years at Saint Basil's Grammar School for Boys?

I certainly learnt the expression *veni, vidi, vici*. Then there was chromatography and the Four Evangelists. I learnt a line from Paul Verlaine – *il pleure dans mon coeur comme il pleut sur la ville*, I learnt the Irish words for things on the kitchen table, the Hail Mary in German, where the Maginot Line went, bits of *Hamlet*, e=mc2, a heap of songs, how to gate-vault, something about burning magnesium and not much else. That's about the height of it in a nutshell.

But then I never paid much attention in class anyway. The teachers paid no attention either. There might be a big magpie sitting at the window and nobody would even notice. There was a sparrow-hawk just sitting there one day and the teacher threw the duster at me and told me not to be looking at some stupid bird and to get back to whatever he was supposed to be teaching me. And it was a sparrowhawk! Eating a sparrow!

Not every day of the week you see that.

The only class where I was even half awake was the art class although I soon tired of sketching apples. Red apples, green apples, sliced apples, peeled apples. After a while I could just draw apples out of my head and even when I saw Cézanne's apples I was still fed up with them. There was no sport in painting apples. Anybody could paint apples in their sleep. Same went for lemons, peppers and cabbages.

And so the teacher got me to draw the boy sitting beside me but soon I got tired of him too. He had thin lips and a watery eye and he wasn't too pleased with the finished picture. The teacher was charmed, however, and gave me ten out of ten and made me draw everybody in the class and sent me home with a bagful of art books.

Them's very dear books, the granny said. Go and wash your hands.

I didn't let the granny see the books because I knew they were full of nudie women although most of them weren't very sexy nudie women at all. Most of them were big fat lumps, but there were a couple of dishy ones all the same – especially the sculptures with the nipples. I liked them the best.

There was other stuff in the books too and I looked at all the pictures by Van Gogh and Matisse and Soutine and I thought they were good. I didn't like Picasso very much at all and the teacher was disappointed because he thought Picasso was the bee's knees. The ones I liked best were the Fauves – the wild beasts – the mad bastards – and I wanted to be one of them. The teacher told me I'd have to wait until after my exams and that then I could be as mad as I liked. He said that I would be an Expressionist but in the meantime, I'd be as well to paint the vegetables and the fruit. I told him that I wanted to paint nudie women like one of the ones in *The Romans of the Decadence* but he said that there wasn't much likelihood of that at Saint Basil's. There were no nudie women in Fermanagh and I only got a C in my O level.

SOME TULIP

The guilt is a curse. It's the worst curse of all and it began to get the better of me all of a sudden – bang in the middle of a painting. I was, at the time, once again attempting to reproduce a likeness of the Infant of Prague and was succeeding moderately in a loose and expressionistic sort of a way. The little man was appearing to float in a landscape of browns, greens and purples – blanket bog perhaps in the far and windy west.

Anyway, it was all going quite well when suddenly I began to shiver and fret about the Maguire woman and how she had stolen the real thing from the city of Prague. I began to think aloud and while this was bad enough in itself, the subsequent deception had been worse again. Weren't the innocent pilgrims of Prague presently praying to an Action Man? And wasn't the stolen goods in all his finery, at this very moment, up in a side altar in the church at home?

I resolved to make amends. Only with the relief of honest restitution would I be able to lose my jittery guilt, the cold nocturnal sweats and the hawkshead moths who were constantly headbutting the lining of my stomach. I would do whatever I could to return the statue to its rightful place in the capital of the former Czechoslovakia.

This was easier said than done. The local clergy would have none of it.

Let the hare sit, said the big priest from Clones.

Ah sure I wouldn't know anything about that, said the wee priest from Carrickmacross.

Don't look at me, I just work here, muttered the new priest from Monaghan town.

They were no use at all. Anything for a quiet life. No fuss. No palaver. Don't wake the Bishop.

And so I phoned the Bishop at four in the morning but only got his secretary – although I think it really was the Bishop pretending to be his secretary so that he wouldn't have to talk to me. Anyway, he said the Bishop wasn't available and that he would be sure and tell him of my concerns and that maybe I should put it in writing. But I'm not stupid. The Bishop was only trying to juke me and so I knew I had to take the matter to a higher authority.

Dear Holy Father,

You don't know me but when you were in Galway you said that you loved the young people of Ireland. I wasn't there that day because the housekeeper in the priests' house said that I was too young to go and I couldn't get a place on the bus. I ended up going to Knock with the grandmother and it rained the whole day. To tell you the truth I wouldn't go across the road to see you nowadays but I was very young then and had no wit.

Anyway, just writing to tell you that the real Child of Prague is in a side altar in the church up the town. The one in Prague is an Action Man. The Feds know it, the nuns know it and over here, the dogs in the street know it. I don't know if you know yourself but I'm just letting you know because the priests of the parish won't listen to me. I think they reckon I'm not the full whack. Please get on the blower to the Bishop and tell him to get the finger out. It's a disgrace that the people in Prague are praying to an Action Man and it's about time that the stolen statue went home. I was going to write to Jimmy Savile but I thought you'd be the man – only joking, your Holiness! HA! HA! About Jimmy Savile, I mean. I'm dead serious about the Child of Prague though.

Best wishes,

A young person of Ireland.

PS I saw you with Bob Dylan. He's some tulip, isn't he!

Of course I binned this letter as soon as I had written it. The tone was wrong. After all, I was trying to make an impression on him so I wrote another one which was all respectful and polite. Not that it mattered much anyway. I knew there was hardly much chance of the Pope getting the letter anyway. If I couldn't even get a hold of the Bishop I'd hardly have much chance with the Chief Bombardier himself. I knew that some pot-bellied cardinal would probably read it first and then just chuck it in the bin because the Pope was far too busy for letters from the likes of me.

What with all the travelling and the praying and the pontificating, there's not enough hours in the day.

And so I forgot all about that particular letter for a while and, in the meantime, fired off other ones left, right and centre. I wrote about four to the local MP, three to the local council, one to the local convent and about twenty or so to the local papers. I was quite the letter-writer. By the end of the week I could have written letters in my sleep. Even so, only the convent replied – some wee nun sent me a little prayer which I was supposed to say three times a day – the way you'd take a cough bottle.

I was naturally very disheartened by the lack of interest but I vowed that I would continue to write as many letters as I could and that I would say the prayer three times a day. And what do you think happened? My prayers were answered! As true as I'm sitting here talking to this wall.

There I was watching the news and there suddenly was the Pope himself looking out the big window of the Vatican and all these thousands of Polish nuns smiling up at him and waving and what do you think he does? Out from under his vestments he whips the letter! Then he leans into the microphone with a big face on him and, in a booming voice, he starts reading my letter out to all the people down below! They are clapping and cheering at the end of every sentence but he looks very serious indeed.

It was only on the television for a few seconds and it was quite hard to make out, what with the newsreader talking all over it and the Pope's microphone Latin. But it was my letter all right. I was certain sure of that much,

And so, after that, I lived in a little hope that something might be done about the Child of Prague which was still standing in the side altar looking at everybody as if to say –

Yous should be ashamed of yourselves. Yous know rightly and the poor grandmother in her grave!

But nothing happened at all. Nobody paid a blind bit of attention to the Pope at all and the local clergy said that they hadn't even seen the news that day because the television was on the blink. Of course, the Bishop remained inaccessible even though, in my next letter, I gave him a sharp reminder of the whole notion of schism and asked him what was the point of the Pope saying things if nobody even bothered to watch the news? There was no response. I complained to the Vatican about the Bishop. Again there was no response. Maybe it had gone to the wrong address?

Nevertheless, I kept up the letter-writing. A few determined letters every day, but, even so, nothing was happening as far as I could see – unless there was something going on behind the scenes and the Child might soon be handed over at the border in exchange for the Action Man. And so I blarged on and continued to say the prayer three times a day and just kept at it. The grandmother always said that you had to keep at it no matter what it was.

Keep at it, son, she would say, God loves a trier.

★   ★   ★

Ornithological interlude:

The chough or *Pyrrhocorax pyrrhocorax* is a crow with a red beak that flaps about the coast of Donegal in spectacular flocks as if they are showing off to the tourists. Although the chough is hard to miss, a novice might easily mistake one for a jackdaw or a rook. This might perhaps explain why I never saw one until this week even though I have been seeing them all of my life. There was maybe even a flock of choughs wheeling and diving as head-the-ball the fossil man was tumbling into the foam.

The grandmother never really wanted me to paint her at all, but when I showed her a picture of Saint Catherine of Siena in one of her ecstasies she was suddenly delighted with the idea. She saw the value in being portrayed as saintly given the events that had happened when she was alive – the miracle cures and the crowds leaning on her hedge. It was also an opportunity for us to talk and I had something very important to ask her.

I sat her on a chair in the corner of the room and hung a blue velvet drape behind her. The light was good and her face looked noble and serene. I asked her to arrange her hands upon her lap and, once settled, she held them as if in casual prayer. I hung the picture of Saint Catherine of Siena in her eyeline so that she might have something to look at and I requested that she keep as still as possible.

Are you comfortable enough there, Granny?

Sure how would I be comfortable here and not a

child in the house washed? Don't make me look too old now!

What age are you, Granny?

I'm twenty-one.

And so I began to paint the grandmother, squaring up to the thing, my eyes half closed as I studied her tones from behind my eyelashes. I pressed my tongue hard against my bottom teeth and I breathed heavily through my nose as it all began to come together very quickly indeed. The wonderful sensation of working fast and loose gave me the confidence to bring it up again.

So how are you, Granny? I asked as I knuckled out another slug of yellow ochre.

I'm grand, son. That was a big funeral.

It was. You're a popular woman.

I must have been surely, she smiled.

Granny, do you remember the business in Bundoran?

Her eyes suddenly shot away from Saint Catherine of Siena and then fixed on mine.

Whist! she said, not a word about it. You'll get us all lifted! Every one of us will end up in the Barracks!

But, Granny, I said, trying to be relaxed about it, you always believed me, didn't you? About the man . . . and me hitting him with the hammer and . . .

I don't want to hear another word about it!

But you did believe me, didn't you?

Of course I believed you, she said impatiently.

And then, deep in memory, she looked back towards

Saint Catherine of Siena and, almost inaudibly, whispered the words –
    Didn't it run in the family?

CRUMBS

The grandmother's story was an extraordinary one. So extraordinary perhaps that it might even be prefaced with *Once upon a time* or *fadó fadó*. It certainly might pass as some class of fairy story to my mind. But the question is whether or not you'd believe me if I was to tell you what the grandmother told me? I doubt if you would. But I must tell you that she was never ever one for the fairy stories herself. In fact, she had never told me a fairy story in her whole life.

That's only oul' pistrix! she would say. Only oul nonsense to frighten childer.

But she did believe in the fairies themselves and believed in them just as much as she believed in the holy wells and the holy saints. In fact, she would regularly attribute certain events to their specific influence.

Case in point. The bizarre death of my primary school teacher Master Evans – something which to this day I'm very sorry I missed, me being at the bogs when it happened. On my return, however, I discovered that everyone in the class was throwing books and paper aeroplanes all over the place and that Master Evans, the old bastard, was lying on his jelly-belly in a big pool of his own blood. He had been impaled on a giant compass after falling off the nature table. A freak accident they called it.

But this was to prove no mystery to the grandmother, however. Not in the slightest. And she was fit to explain the whole thing with the revelation that, in order to erect one of those spider's-web garden clothes lines, Master Evans had recently cut down a fairy thorn at the back of his house. Oh, he should have known better, she said, but he went ahead anyway because they had told him at teacher training college that there was no such a thing as the fairies.

And that, she said, had been his big mistake. For what do you think was lying on that very nature table? Bits of that very fairy thorn! The same fairy thorn that he had attacked with the hedge clippers and the chainsaw! Now I ask you, she said, what do you make of that?

The grandmother would also sometimes claim to have actually seen the fairies herself with her own two eyes. They were, she used to tell me with great seriousness, playing on a building site out near the Round O. It was a spring evening, she said, and she heard them singing and playing tunes and she thought she would take a wee peep. Then, when she quietly peered through a rough hoarding to get her wee peep, there they were – half a dozen little people hashing away to themselves in a strange language.

But whether you believe the thing or not is neither here nor there. The grandmother's word was good enough for me. And always was. Consequently, I have no doubt whatsoever in my mind that the following story related to me (as I attempted to make a portrait painting of herself) is absolute gospel, the honest truth and a real tale – a story which is entirely confident in the factual horror of itself.

The granny was in the kitchen doing the ironing and having terrible trouble with the frayed collar of the father's working shirt. He was in the parlour reading the death notices in the *Irish News* and picking at his teeth with folded corners of newsprint. It was a dark Saturday and the moo-moos had been spared the effects of his hammer for the weekend. This arrangement suited everyone except, it seems, the mother who had been trying all morning to rise a row. She was, at this time, poking vigorously at the Aga and had a big face on her.

The grandmother said that it was always like this. The daughter-in-law (the mother) was in the kitchen and the father was in the parlour with the *Irish News*. I, being only three, was in my usual position under the table, shaking the legs of the chairs and trying to catch clock beetles and slaters with my chubby fingers. I was always a good cub, she said, and I was as happy as the day was long pottering about under the table with my playmates the bugs.

As she gave me these details, I immediately began to remember that old feeling of being under that table surrounded by the legs of the chairs and the table itself. It was a strange mixture of being both secure and trapped and I remembered the sheltered cosiness of it. Secure and yet trapped – institutionalised they would call it now – like working for the Civil Service or the BBC.

And I could all of a sudden remember the smell of the lino and its design of lines and squares – like Mondrian or the patterns we would learn to draw on graph paper at the wee boys' school where the Master Evans would one day be killed after falling off the nature table because he cut down the fairy thorn at the back of the house.

And as the grandmother continued her story I continued to paint the tones of her beautiful face. Bit by bit she was developing on the canvas before me, and bit by bit her story began to get more and more heart-thumping and uneasy. She told me that she had never liked the mother because she was bad to the moo-moo-slaughtering father and him with a good job in the abattoir. She said that the mother was never any good in the first place and that her whole connection was no good either. And it went both ways too. The mother had even less time for the grandmother. The father just stayed out of it and read the *Irish News* from top to bottom.

On this occasion, however, as the grandmother pressed the hissing iron on the frayed collar of the father's working shirt, a row started. The mother, according to the grandmother, was complaining about the Aga and insisting that she wanted a proper cooker like the one in Kerr's window up the town and said that she was fed up boiling water all day on our old-fashioned lump of a thing.

The grandmother, of course, swore by the Aga – it was her altar and she stood before it daily, wiping it, polishing it and sometimes just staring at it. And look at the price you'd give for an Aga nowadays, she said – big money – but in them days, the mother was never done complaining about it and the grandmother's head was bealded.

As I worked away at getting the grandmother's eyes right, I realised that they were exactly like my own. Same blue, same lines, same crow's feet. I knew my own eyes well from doing the odd self-portrait on those days when I could think of nothing else to paint.

And it's an exercise a painter has to do – to stare at his own face in a mirror and really see what he looks like himself – to scrutinise yourself as if you are somebody else and then move your gaze objectively between the canvas and the person in the mirror with his hair split on the opposite side to yours. Self-portraits are scary things. All portraits are scary things – but self-portraits are the scariest of all.

But anyway, the grandmother's portrait was coming along great and she was great at the keeping still. Not a budge out of her – even as the fairy story suddenly changed its shape and transformed into the horror story.

The father came into the kitchen looking for a bit of bread and butter. In those days he was fond of the heel of the loaf and might spend a good hour chewing away to himself as he read the *Irish News*. The mother told him to get it himself but then, when he couldn't find the breadknife, there was a whole fuss and the mother gave out yards about having to show him where it was.

The breadknife was a big ancient and worn breadknife with a bone handle that had been gripped and brandished for a hundred years. An heirloom of sorts – an antique, the grandmother used to say. Next thing the mother was off again complaining about how she had to do everything in the house herself and how the father could do nothing for himself and how he was tied to the grandmother's apron strings and what kind of a man he was and so on. Yap. Yap. Yap. Yap. Yap. Yap. Yap.

And all the time I'm under the table with the creatures of the kitchen and peering out at the increasing racket and noise. Then there was more trouble because the father cut the bread against his overalls instead of on the breadboard and then he complained that the butter was as hard as a rock.

The mother then began to add to her abusive remarks about the father by clattering all the pots and pans – her turned-away face in the dark cave above the Aga as she banged away there like Vulcan in drag. And all the time the father stood there in a pool of breadcrumbs, the antique breadknife pointing in the vague direction of the mother like some strange waving instrument of divination.

I twigged almost immediately that this story was only going the one way. Just like getting the punchline of a long joke a split second before the teller actually reveals it, my mind suddenly lurched forward and completed this murder picture for itself. Jesus, Mary and Joseph! The father had killed the mother. With the breadknife! And I had seen it happen when I was only three and under the kitchen table with the clocks! Is it any wonder I am the way I am? Everything suddenly *explicado*!

Although the grandmother continued to talk away there, I couldn't hear a word of it. I was lost in the nightmare of sudden revelation that the news was bad – very bad – and that nothing whatever could be done. This was as terrible a situation as anybody could ever contemplate and it began to get worse by the second. Imagine the punch in the guts – horrific *coup de grâce* so to speak – as I then heard the grandmother say, quite viciously, the following seven words –

And we buried her in the garden.

Never before had the word *garden* attacked my brain with such force. It became a word like *hammer* or *bomb*. The word was *garden* and with its quick utterance I was sucked suddenly out of my first horror and dropped mercilessly into another. *Garden. Garden. Garden.* And we buried her in the *garden*. They had buried the mother in the *garden*! Like Elvis in Graceland. Like the whale in Bundoran, the mother was buried with the goldfish out among the dandelions and the daisies.

This was indeed shocking and extraordinary and I ceased any further attempts at portraiture almost immediately.

And what this surely meant was that the mother

had not in fact run away with Popeye the Sailor Man?

No, she never did, agreed the grandmother solemnly.

And surely, therefore, all talk of the mother being over in England and having abandoned me and the unmentionable sister was all nonsense?

Again the grandmother agreed and impatiently insisted that she be allowed to finish her story.

But I had too many questions for any story to be able to continue in these circumstances. The moo-moo-slaughtering father, The father? The mother? The breadknife? And not a word was said? And the mother quietly interred at the back of the house? In the *garden*?

The grandmother got ratty.

Well, we couldn't very well say anything about it or we'd all have been lifted! And who'd have reared you then? Tell me that!

And so, out of the blue, there it was. The missing link. It seemed that murder ran in the family like big ears and crooked toes – and so for that matter did burying things. And what more classic a background, I ask you, from which to explain my own murderous enterprises? The father had killed the mother and she had fallen on the Mondrian lino and her head had bounced at the very spot where I, the cub, was busy trying to pin down slaters with the tip of my finger. Memory began to flicker.

From under the table I had watched them drag her out through the scullery and into the dark, dripping,

147

glistening garden where I would later, for years, play tig and Swingball all by myself. And the blood on the lino and the grandmother on the two knees mopping and scrubbing and covering everything up with sheets of the *Irish News*.

And not a word out of the father who had dug himself a hole in record time and tipped the mother's body all wrapped in tarpaulin into the damp, blue-brown, fudgy earth. And, the awful job done, the father said 'game ball' and the grandmother remarked that the garden looked as good as new.

I told the grandmother that the portrait would have to wait but she just said that I should have a titter of wit.

Soon I began to remember the whole episode – the whispered panic in the coal shade and the rattle of garden implements as they searched for the spade. I remembered the blue Scholls the mother was wearing, I remembered the ironing board and the iron and the Child of Prague up on the bedroom windowsill looking down on the whole business with his head Sellotaped on crooked.

And everything began to make sense. That was why the grandmother had always objected to any new spiderweb clothes line for the middle of the garden and why for years she had resisted my endless requests for Swingball and would never let me dig for worms out the back. And that, of course, was why any time a sniffing dog came anywhere near the place she would scream like a peahen and hurl a bin lid at it.

I sat on the floor in front of the unfinished portrait

of the grandmother. She sat in front of me tutting and muttering something which was intended to indicate that she couldn't see what I was so upset about, but I just sat there looking around me and sighing. I began to stare at the stern incomplete face of the grandmother that peered back from the canvas – a ghostly image of herself wearing my own two eyes floating there unsatisfied between myself and herself.

I tried to think straight. I could now remember everything but it couldn't possibly be true? I had to try to be sure that those memories were real – not some memory of something I had imagined, or some instant thought that came to me as memory. But one thing was for certain sure – if either the grandmother or myself had not somehow invented this scene and the father really *had* killed the mother, then much was suddenly and very obviously, as I said before in Spanish, *explicado*.

And so, cautiously, I asked the grandmother if there was any possibility that she might be imagining things. She was, of course, immediately indignant and began to angrily smooth her skirt as she always did when expressing offence. Trying to redeem the situation I put it to her that it was a very hard thing for me to hear – that I had been playing Swingball on the mother's grave and that it was the moo-moo-slaughtering father who had dispatched her with the antique breadknife. At that the grandmother at once began to shake her head wildly and stamp the heel of her shoe on the boards of the floor –

No! No! No! No! she hissed impatiently. What are you hashing about, son? The father killed the mother? Not at all! Sure he wouldn't hurt a fly that fella! Sure he wouldn't have it in him to get rid of that one. Not at all, son, you have it all barways, so you have!

For the briefest of moments I felt a sudden sharp relief. Maybe somehow I had misheard, misunderstood and misconstrued? Somehow I had picked her up wrong and those recovered memories of lino and blood and clay were not memories at all? And maybe the mother was in England after all, eating the spinach with Popeye the Sailor Man?

So, I asked, the father did *not* kill the mother?

No he did not indeed! she replied. Are you mad?

So she's in England with a sailor?

Are you not listening to me, son? She's buried in the bloomin' garden!

So the father *did* kill her?

How many times do I have to tell you? It wasn't the father who killed her!

Well, for God's sake, Granny, who killed her?

Are you stupid or what? she spat, her voice rising as she stood up. It was *me*! I killed her! With the iron! Isn't that what I'm trying to tell you! It was *me* who killed her! Hit her full whack on the back of the head with the iron – a ton weight it was – it would give you a quare bang.

HA! HA!

I have no real memories of the mother although after the grandmother's tale I am, in odd moments of sleep, inclined to see once again the Aga and the lino and the hasty burial. I still cannot picture the mother's face apart from some cartoon version of herself sneaking out the back door to meet Popeye and head for England on his steamboat. In fact, I knew nothing of the mother apart from what the grandmother had told me and her views were clearly jaundiced.

The grandmother, at our next sitting, went on to tell me many things. Not only did she hate the mother but she hated all the other sons – the uncles. They were, she said, a shower of shites. She cared only for the father because he was a hard worker and he was the only one who could ever have been trusted after the incident with the iron.

She further confessed that she no more believed in God than the man in the moon, although she would never admit it to anyone. Nor did she believe in Heaven or Hell. She did, however, have great faith in the saints and she said that one day she would become one herself and that in ten years' time I was to dig her up and check. She bet me a fiver that she would be preserved there like a lump of bog butter and that the clergy would start a whole palaver. Other than that she said she only believed in stones and wells and the Child of Prague.

Then more family history . . .

The mother, she said, was always bad news. She had delusions about herself. She thought she was God's gift. Mad in the head. Sometimes she would think that the house was full of cats. Another time she wouldn't go near the father because she thought he was the Devil! She was a hard woman to live with – as mad as get out.

Do you not remember, son, the way she always used to pull the breadknife on the poor father? Ah now, she had us all astray in the head. And then we had to bury her in the garden on account of all the checkpoints in them days. We wouldn't have got half a mile down the road with her on the bar of the bike.

And so it was clear to me that I had a murderous history. We were a dynasty no less. A long line. I had killed the Bundoran man, the father had killed the moo-moos, the mother had attempted to kill the father and the grandmother had killed the mother. Who knows what happened further back? Maybe even the *great*-grandmother had dispatched somebody too – one of the neighbours or a visiting missionary perhaps? And then there had always been that story about my great-great-grandfather being hanged in the Broad Meadow – so obviously he must have bumped somebody off too. Some sheep-stealing enterprise no doubt.

The grandmother's story had a huge effect on me. It was then for the first time that I started to worry about myself and lose the plot a little. It was around that time that I began to believe that I was being constantly watched, followed and pursued. Every time I saw the dark bulletproof glass of a cop car glide past, its windows full of reflections, I would feel a sudden upheaval in the stomach.

If I saw the same person twice in the one day I would panic. As I walked in the city I was always convinced I was being followed by all manner of plain-clothes figures – and as soon as my follower would disappear into a shop I would assume him replaced by another and another and so on. And so I would retrace my steps and wait for my pursuer to approach, daring him to speak as he came close. I would stare him in the eye and challenge him to reveal himself – but he never would. Too clever for that. Too well trained – and he would wander nonchalantly on. Then I would feel sick and I would go round the corner to sit on my hunkers and boke all over my gutties.

The drink would have me jangly too – all nervy and despairing as I thought about the back garden and them all stamping on the ground, sowing the grass seed, waiting edgily for it to grow and me hammering the Swingball pole into the very same spot – and the poor goldfish buried there too – their bodies and bones wasting like little anchovies in the clay.

But then hadn't the grandmother said that the

mother was deluded? Maybe I was deluded too? And maybe I was just seeing things when I thought I was being followed? It wasn't necessarily the Branch or Interpol or Carmelite nuns or anybody for that matter. Might have been nothing at all. But even so.

And wasn't painting itself all to do with seeing things? Representing something that you have seen in your mind's eye – at least that's the way I do it. It was different when I had to paint the apples and the cabbages, but nowadays what am I doing only representing some kind of vision? For instance, a coot is *not* yellow. So why do I paint a coot yellow? And for the person looking at it? How do you know it's a coot even though it doesn't look like a coot? The bloody thing is the wrong colour for a start.

And then how do we know, any of us, that we see things the way another person does? They say there was something wrong with El Greco's eyes that made him see people so long and spidery and doleful. But then maybe there is something wrong with my eyes, or your eyes, and maybe El Greco is right? Maybe we do actually look like that? It's a conundrum all right – so don't talk to me about seeing things.

Delusions, they say. That's all they are. Talking to people who aren't there, hearing voices that aren't there. And what about all these religious people who believe in the invisible? What's all that about? And what's the difference, if you don't mind me asking, in talking to Harvey the Rabbit and talking to the Patron Saint of Rabbits when neither of them is actually in the room with you? And if you actually *see* Harvey the Rabbit or the Patron Saint of Rabbits then you are seeing things that *aren't there*.

This sort of thing used to keep me awake at nights and I didn't sleep much for about six months just worrying about it all. And the only thing for sure was that I could certainly see why the grandmother had never had any difficulty in believing that the cub (the grandson) had done what he had. It was as likely as anything else that he too might crack someone on the back of the head with some class of implement – an iron, a hammer, a bin lid.

No great leap involved in crediting such a thing when you had already done it yourself. And anyway, she probably knew by my face. It was there that she could see her own murderous eyes looking back at her – contemplating her – anxiously meditating on delusions – of grandeur – of grandma – ha! ha!

MISTER TOM JONES

One wet morning at St Basil's Grammar School for young bucks, I was illegally warming myself at the pipes and thinking away to myself about all manner of things – waterhens, sparrowhawks, redwings and the mute swan. It was a normal enough morning – everyone was soaking wet and the cold air was full of sick moisture.

This was a damp and steaming land of condensation and I thought for a moment that I was in a laundry where my entire spirit might be dry-cleaned for ever. Here, in this comfortless purgatory, they had no regard for the leaping hare, the chunky bullfinch or the hawthorn hedge. Here, they cared for nothing at all.

The teacher in first class was as poisonous as ever – sitting there drooling in front of the three-bar electric fire and the big coat and the pasty carcass of him all sickly primed with oily coffee and nicotine. No walking to school in any monsoon downpour for him. No wet trousers clinging to his blue thighs.

I think it all really started when Mister Balls (let's call him Mister Balls) finally had his daily brainwave and had, with great effort, come up with something for us all to do. He always gave us a composition, that was a given, but the difficulty for him had always been to come up with a subject. He used to think about this for the first half an hour of the class, sitting there with his head in his hands and his shins getting hotter by the second in front of the three-bar electric fire. It seemed to take it out of him.

Not that it ever really mattered much anyway because he always came up with something really boring like 'A Day in the Countryside' or 'A Trip to the Seaside'. On this day, however, he came up with what he probably thought was a cracker – 'My Father's Occupation'. The heart sank immediately. As the rest of the class began to scrawl out the stories of their fathers, I pondered in some pain just how exactly I should put it – the glorious fact that the father was the Great Slayer of the Moo-Moos?

Anyway, whatever, I went about my task in great secrecy, making a stockade of my elbows, hands and arms and leaning into that breathy darkness with my tongue sticking out of the side of my mouth. Soon enough I had completed the page and had quietly begun to slumber full of helpless delicious sleep on the slabbery pillow of my forearm. It was, however, to be a short-lived oblivion. Next thing I knew I had been clattered on the crown of the head with a box of chalk. Mister Balls might well have been the most useless bollocks that ever walked, but he was a marksman even so.

I woke up to laughter and confusion. Then there was the jeering and the dead old voice of Mister Balls summoning me to the front of the class –

the very last place I wanted to be. Apart from the presence of the three-bar electric fire, the front of the class was a truly desolate and hopeless place. It was also an entirely lawless territory where any lost soul might suddenly be clouted, punched, strapped, choked or otherwise humiliated without any right to self-defence whatsoever. And so I walked to the front like the condemned man that I was – the jury of my own peers all suddenly excited at the ugly possibilities of it all.

Have a nice wee sleep, did you? says Mister Balls, apparently addressing his remarks to the light bulb.

I said nothing. It was impossible in these circumstances to say anything that would not be used against you.

I take it you have completed your composition? he whined, again looking towards the light bulb, perhaps you'd like to share it with the class?

Teachers always said things like that. Perhaps you'd like to *share* it with the class. And you felt like saying, no I don't feel like sharing it with the fucking class! But you never did. You couldn't say anything because you didn't know the right words in those days. In those days I only knew words like *moo-moo* and *flip off!* and the minute I started to read the whole class started laughing and coughing and choking and wetting themselves and old Mister No Teaching Qualifications Whatsoever began to feel very proud of himself indeed,

My father kills *moo-moos!* he repeated sneering, at

the . . . the . . . *aba* . . . the *abbey*something? And what is this word if you please?

If you please! That was another one like *share it with the class!* No I don't *please!* And yes it is *too much trouble!* And no I can't spell *abattoir!* How am I supposed to know how to spell *abattoir* – I'm not a fucking Frenchman! I'm only twelve years old for fuck's sake!

If only they had seen me during break-time. When Mister Balls was off warming the backs of his legs against the staffroom, when the boys were out in the yard hanging from drainpipes, spitting, and kicking each other. If only they had seen me then – once again in the empty classroom of Mister Balls – standing there with the two legs wide apart, the two hands gripping the flex of the three-bar electric fire and me swinging it, still glowing, around my head in an ever increasing orbit. And me singing at the top of my lungs a song called 'It's Not Unusual' – a hit for Mister Tom Jones, the popular Welshman.

THE FISH'S HAND

And in the paper they have found a fossil hand. It's belonging to a fish. More a jointed fin than a hand but even so. They say that it indicates the way a fish might first have dragged itself on to dry land – long before the monkeys – and long before *Homo* anything. That's no bad one. A fish with hands no less! Imagine the shock you'd get if your float began to drag against the current and you took your time to strike and hook your big bronze bream and, sure enough, you felt it pulsing on the line and what suddenly breaks the water but a fishy gub and two big waving hands? You wouldn't be long dropping your rod in the rushes and tearing away off up the bank. A fish with hands would certainly put the heart crossways on me anyway.

And the grandmother would sometimes wonder about a fossil I might show her and ponder on my explanation –

You mean to tell me that this was a creature that was alive millions of years ago in Bundoran?

Yes.

Before there was even a Bundoran?

Yes.

Well, would you credit that? Do you think it was a fish or a snail or a what?

Probably some kind of a snail or something very like it.

Well, God save us! Isn't it wonderful altogether!

And still I watched and still I painted and still I wondered about everything that had happened. Especially, I have to say, about the murders, about the Child of Prague and about beautiful Billie Maguire. Apart from that all I did was keep writing the letters.

Dear Shirley Temple,

Who'd have thought you'd ever have ended up in the diplomatic service? Imagine that! And who'd have ever thought you'd have ended up in PRAGUE no less? It's a gorgeous place too, isn't it? That's a great job you have altogether and I'm sure you're on great money. You don't know me but I am an Irish painter and I have for some time been trying to bring something to the attention of the Czechs but they won't take any notice. You are my LAST HOPE! The Child of Prague has been STOLEN and were you to go down to the church this minute and take a look and say to yourself, no, it hasn't been stolen at all because there it is, STILL in its glass case, you'd be very WRONG. You see, Mrs Temple, that thing in the glass case is not the real Child of Prague at all but rather an ACTION Man – a kind of soldier doll – I don't know if you had them in America ever? I think the Czechs know damn well but won't do anything about it and the nuns are probably afraid to say BOO TO A GOOSE. Please do something about this scandalous scenario. Thanking you. The grandmother will be charmed that I have written to you although she always thought you were very oul'-fashioned for your age and a bit of a wee madam. Anyway, pass no remarks on her. She's DOTING.

Yours faithfully, etc.

And when I had finished my letters for the day, I would paint or maybe think about fossils again. It was strange to think that in millions of years someone would dig up the back garden and find a fossil of the mother with the dint in her skull. And that some scientist would say on the future telly that perhaps one *Homo sapiens* had clouted another with a blunt instrument – maybe a primitive tool or suchlike. They would put her in a museum like the mummy and she would have her constant squealing court of skinhead children in the Ulster Museum.

And we come from the monkeys, you tell me?

That's right, Granny.

You mean like the ones out of the *Tarzan* pictures?

The very men.

And in the paper:

Pericles of Athens has just been dug up – or so it says. According to Mr Yannis Tsedakis, the director of antiquities at the Greek Cultural Ministry, this is one of the most important finds since the war. It's not Pericles exactly but they reckon they have discovered part of the Demosion Sima – his possible last resting place.

Apparently, Pericles and other great men were buried in mass graves called polyandria and they have found at least four polyandria and they know there is a fifth. They've been trying to find this place for years and, in the end, they found it only by chance.

And still the whale, the goldfish and the mother lie in wait for some attentive dig. A crowd of university longhairs down on their knees with their trowels and their paintbrushes.

SHAMPOO

And then I would imagine the washing of the hair. And Billie Maguire tucking a rough yellow towel into the collar of my shirt, and touching the back of my skull with her fingertips, causing me to stoop and direct my nose to the sink. And from there I see the plughole descend into Hell before me and I might think at once of Hitchcock and the bloodswirl of death and murder as the water and suds and bubbles begin to fall.

I stick my fingers in my ears to save them from any soapy invasion and keep my eyes clenched shut, affording to both of them some similar protection. The only other vulnerable spots, the nose and the mouth, are dealt with separately. The mouth can be kept watertight and shut except for occasions of necessary conversation and the nostrils of the nose are adequately proofed thanks to the effects of natural forces, the angle of the head and the laws of physics. I am otherwise comfortable and ready.

Is that water OK? It's not too hot, is it? she asks.

It's fine, I say.

You sure? she says.

Certain sure, I say.

And with that, the hot water begins to flow over

the bump at the back of my head and stream down and down – warm, warm, warm – over the backs of my ears and all over my surrendered neck. I am putting my head on a block for Billie in her leather mask and her almost toppling over with the weight of the axe itself. I think for a moment of the back of my neck and then I stop thinking about anything and simply try to enjoy. The pleasure. The imagining. The entertaining of the thought.

And soon my whole body begins to shiver to every hot little rivulet that escapes on its own and runs under an ear and down the front of my shirt – a shudder and a warm feeling all in one. And the pressure of the shower begins to soothe the muscles underneath the base of my pointy skull and I smile drunkenly to myself for these are the very muscles that I rub when I'm tired or full of murderous tensions and hate. And slowly I begin to relax – my neck, my shoulders and even my hunched-over spine begin to loosen and think of foreign lands.

I manoeuvre my head to that she can push once more into those muscles. And I inhale the smell of her smell and roll my head sideways to the lush lathering in my hair – the pressure of her fingers – the soft crinkled tips, the sharp digging nails.

Are you OK there? she asks.

And I begin to sigh in my mind at the sheer beauty of it, knowing that this is some kind of happiness I experience only on these days when Billie the Spy shows up for the washing of the hair and the rinsing of the suds – an ecstasy only imaginable since she had first knocked like Ingrid Bergman on the comforting door.

She leans closer to my ear and, as she speaks to me with questions of hot water and soap, her voice cuts right through my head – her breath hot, her smell rich – her lips accidentally touching my ear as I shiver and shift in my seat once more. I try to hold the moment longer – her mouth at my ear and the condensation of her breath steaming through my brain.

Her new soft voice swims into the damp cave of my head and my every nerve is charged with lethal electrics – that sudden torrent of rinsing water roaring into one ear and through my soul marking the sudden conclusion as Billie Maguire begins to take less care with the whole thing – no sensitivity left in her hands and the next ritual manoeuvres in the washing of the hair become suddenly rough and unloving.

The shampoo drains and falls in splats in the sink and Billie wraps the towel around my head and begins to scrub – me still hunched over and suddenly aware once more of the stiffness in the back. I begin to force myself against the pressure of her hands and a little loving struggle begins as she urges me to stay where I am for one more minute. And full of old thoughts of the grandmother and the drying of the hair at the kitchen jarbox, I hang the two arms by my side and allow her to jolt my head from side to side with a certain violence and disregard. And there is much I want to tell Billie Maguire in our strange moments of love.

But I don't say anything because I don't trust her any more and, anyway, she always seems impatient these days – tired of me, humouring me sometimes but, more often, just looking at me funny. And there is no point in saying much at the end of the washing of the hair because, with the soapy eyelashes shut tight in fear beneath the lemon towel, I might look like Carmen Miranda.

So here I am talking to the wall once more. It's all I ever seem to do and maybe a sudden rage might overtake me and I might grab the towel from my head and stand up glaring all straggly haired and red-eyed like some madman from a Russian book. And Billie Maguire might stand back frightened as I decide to put on some reckless display.

And I might shout, It's like talking to the fucking wall! If I was in Prague with you I'd have to show you where I kissed some other beautiful woman beneath a stumpy tree and then you would huff and betray me and leave me lonely in the park! And an artist needs his secrets – even his deadly ones – especially his deadly ones! And talking to you is like talking to the fucking wall! I don't love you, Billie Maguire. And you are not my friend!

And Billie Maguire might be suddenly serious and scared. And she might call out as she runs from the room and I would stand there dripping into my own little pool and wait for censure, for questions, for more hoking and poking around in my head as I beg her to come back once more.

I'm sorry, Billie Maguire, I would say, I didn't mean what I said. I'm sorry, Billie Maguire.

And then I might cry like a baby who had lost the mammy.

SEEING THINGS

And so I have a question of my own. Why was it, that when I was finally granted a genuine vision, that it was not one of Matisse or Modigliani or Picasso or Soutine? Why not one of Elvis Presley or the grandmother or the moo-moo-slaughtering father? Why not one of a washed-up whale or the Child of Prague or a heron or a coot? These are questions most mysterious to me and often I attempt to work out the answers to them on late nights and early mornings, lying awake frantic with some kind of unnameable panic.

I was in my studio relaxed. The usual jitters had not kicked in because I was not, as yet, in that advanced state of jangly hangover that always seems to provoke it. I was alone, clear-headed and feeling like a real artist. The studio was untidy but there were signs of great activity all around – pages lay scattered on the floor and a half-empty bottle of St Emilion, the Patron Saint of Rue de Buci's corner café, stood solemnly on a chair.

I was feeling positive, creative and unencumbered by responsibility. I had no outstanding duties, no visits to make to post office or bank and there had been no post in the hallway to distract me with bureaucracy and boredom.

And my nerves felt sharp that day. There seemed to be a fine line around everything in the room and I wanted to paint everything in sight – the bottle, the pile of newspapers and the chair. I even thought about cutting up bits of the paint-splattered floorboards and framing them. And so I stared in great fascination at my familiar floor for what must have been an hour just sipping at the wine and getting more content by the second. And then that curious feeling of contentment made me even more content and, for the first time in a long time I was, quite possibly, happy.

Billie Maguire is not my sister! I yelled for no reason that I could think of, she is not my sister!

I confused myself with that remark so I tried to focus on her and what she meant. What had Billie Maguire ever done, when you think about it, other than bring chaos into my life and insti-gate a potentially disastrous encounter with spooks, spies, detectives, nuns and television producers? She could have got me lifted, charged, jailed, shot and ruined. She might well have been the end of me in every way.

With her gone, I would no longer have to pussyfoot around in my own conscience. With her gone, I would be able to look at a tree on a Prague street and celebrate the night I kissed a beautiful woman and she kissed me back. With her gone, I might return to myself.

If Billie Maguire had come to Prague with me, I could never have told her such things about trees and beautiful women. All wonder and precious memory would have had to remain as secrets lodged so deep that they would eventually have had no meaning whatever and would have faded into nothing – nothing even strong enough for me to smile at in private moments.

And then, with me lying down in the angle where the floor met the wall, came the vision.

What I saw did not so much appear on the far wall but more came through it – indeed through all four walls simultaneously, from all sides and all corners. And yet I was not at all frightened by this extraordinary sight. It was as if a whole gang of old friends had suddenly showed up. And that is exactly what they were – my old friends the saints – arriving all at once through the vaporous walls of my room.

And so you might imagine me on the splattery floor of that room, raising myself up on one elbow and gazing at the saints themselves drifting through the walls and coming to a halt. Saint Martin himself looking more like Sugar Ray Robinson than ever, Saint Patrick all episcopal and green and Saint Joseph of Cupertino up floating around the light bulb. They were all there – Saint Jude, Saint Michael, Saint Anthony and a few others I couldn't name offhand. And I thought to myself that if I only had a camera I'd have got some great pictures – me with my arm around Saint Patrick or whatever.

There wasn't much said, however, and Saint Patrick, as it happened, was the only one who spoke. I imagine that this was probably all to do with simple language barriers – none of them, after all, would have spoken much English. Saint Patrick didn't seem to have much English either but at least we were able to converse in schoolboy Irish, with me employing the meagre vocabulary I had picked up at Saint Basil's Fun Factory. We might perhaps have addressed each other in the Latin but I knew even less of that – apart from *veni, vidi, vici* and the school motto which, come to think of it, I don't actually remember at all – *jiggere, pokere*, something.

By way of painting a picture of the scene – Saint Patrick was all dressed to the nines in green episcopal regalia with a big three-foot mitre balanced dangerously on his head. In one hand he clutched a big brutal crozier and between the finger and thumb of the other he clutched a giant but droopy shamrock. His long beard was curly like wool and, about the eyes, he looked like Ronnie Drew – former singer with the Dubliners, the rowdy but popular Irish ballad group.

In any case, here is a rough translation of my opening exchange with the Patron Saint of Our Isle –

PATRICK, THE APOSTLE OF IRELAND: Still at the painting?
MYSELF: I am indeed. You still at the pigs?
PATRICK, THE APOSTLE OF IRELAND: Ha ha.
MYSELF: Tell me this, Saint Patrick? You see, when you were up on the mountain? You used to hear voices, didn't you?

PATRICK, THE APOSTLE OF IRELAND: Sure I'm always hearing voices!
MYSELF: Isn't that what I've been saying all along! Oh look, there's a snake! Only joking, ha ha.
PATRICK, THE APOSTLE OF IRELAND: Ha ha, yourself!

As the rest of the saints looked on and laughed among themselves, myself and the Patron Saint of Ireland had a grand chat. I told him about the Child of Prague and he told me not to worry my head about it because, after all, wasn't it Billie Maguire who had done the actual thieving and hadn't I done my best with all my writing to Shirley Temple and the *Irish Times* and the *Impartial Reporter* and even to the Pope in Rome? (He rolled his eyes when he mentioned the Pope and everybody thought this was hilarious – especially Saint Joseph of Cupertino who began to whizz about at great speed and everybody had to duck.)

Saint Patrick did however express his grave disapproval when I mentioned my murder of the palaeontologist in Bundoran but that done, we amiably discussed fossils and, in particular, ammonites which are commonly considered to be headless snakes turned to stone by Saint Hilda. I told him that in voodoo rituals, the feast of Damballa the Snake God was celebrated on Saint Patrick's Day and he said that it sounded a damn sight better than the parade in New York. He also joked that the grandmother was a bit of a pagan and that he obviously hadn't done much of a job in Fermanagh. He should never have turned around at Tempo.

The rest of them (with the exception of the Flying Friar) just stood around looking serene and it was the happiest day of my life – just me and my friends the saints shooting the breeze. I asked them all to look after the grandmother and they said they would. I asked them to look after me and they said they would do that as well. For once, full of peaceful ease, I lay against the wall and sipped away at the warm St Emilion. They had never heard of him.

THOUGHT FOR THE DAY

And in the paper:

Assisi is wrecked altogether. Earthquake. Priceless frescoes shatter and crumble. Giotto and Cimabue in bits as the first rattle hits the Basilica of Saint Francis. In a year's time, the papers will talk of a resurrection.

These days the saints never come back at all. The grandmother is now only a rare visitor and as for Billie Maguire – she might as well be dead to the world for all I see of her. It is a quiet time and all I do is try to come up with ideas and read the paper. Not a whole lot of worthwhile painting has been done recently, although I am reasonably happy with a series of heads I have just completed for a show in London.

There are thirteen of them and the show is simply called *Mixed Media* – each image inspired by some horrific creation I have encountered in the media 'world'. They are particularly ugly heads I must say – mixed media, as you might expect, and abnormally large in scale. In fact, the show is on at the minute and has been particularly well received.

Now and again I wonder about Billie Maguire's documentary and whether or not it will ever see the light of day. It seems unlikely now, given that The

Cockroach is dead and there is no glory to be had. Just as well because God knows what I said in it. And then there was the editing process to be gone through – and the stupid music they would lay over it.

And so I worked away at painting odds and ends and trying to come up with something coherent and satisfying. But all that ever seemed to appear were ugly heads and birds and whales and saints and landscapes which might have been Parisian in tone, maybe Prague in form, but definitely Bundoran in feel.

And so, the only coherence I could ever find in my ideas and my work was just that – Bundoran. I was clearly obsessed with its rocks, its soapy waves, its secrets and the prospect of return. Certainly it wasn't very far to go, but, in its own way, Bundoran was, to me, a million miles away. Nothing is as easy as it was in those innocent days when I was a cub and palaeontologists scrambled over Roguey and toppled into the sea.

Other times, too tired to work, I would just sit there and look at the unfinished portrait of the grandmother and wonder how it could ever be properly completed. And yet maybe it was already a fine portrait in itself – all ochre and empty spaces and definitely her about the eyes – the beloved grandmother who had killed the mother, the saintly grandmother who was preserved like bog butter up in the boneyard beyond.

And so I decided to leave it as it was – sketchy and unfinished. I decided that it would form part of my next big show, hanging there among the birds and the whales and the saints and the rocky landscapes – almost a holy picture – ferocious and dark and described only with the letters N. F. S.

PILGRIMAGE

It had been a very long time since the smell of Bundoran seaweed had last crept through the hairs of my nose. It had been a very long time since I had sighed deeply at the sight of the vast green marble-topped sea as it appeared on the horizon through the chimney pots and aerials. It had been a very long time since I had felt the excitement of funfairs and candyfloss and ordinary people taken out of themselves and wearing the bright clothes they wouldn't wear at home.

Apart from Billie Maguire, there was only a scattering of men on the bus and nobody said a word the whole way there. Some of them didn't even look out the windows at the hedge, but now and again Billie would look at me and smile as I sat all charmed like a nine-year-old who couldn't wait for the feel of the sand and the thrill of freezing water rising around his middle as he shuddered and gasped and held his arms above him like the wings of a skinny bird. Whenever Billie looked over at me, I would smile back and wave across at her.

For years people had taken the bus to Bundoran and now at last it was Billie Maguire and me. This would be our special day and she would skip though the marram in her white dress and we would lie on a blanket over by Roguey Rock and eat sweets and I would watch the wind blow through her hair as she closed her eyes in the sunshine. Inside my head I was, for once, as happy as a merry-go-round. Soon I would paint her all lapis lazuli on the rocks.

Suddenly, the bus turned a corner, pointed itself at the ocean and stopped. The driver lit a cigarette and we all got off. Most people headed for the streets and the slot machines and the holy statues in the windows, but I ran straight down the bank and on to the sand which pressed up against my feet like the surface of a whole new planet. Around me men and women lay astonished in the sunshine – men with their arms over their eyes, their shirts off and the buttons of their trousers open at the waist, red-faced women with white legs watching their children bury each other in the damp sand all cruelly hacked up around them. And I stepped silently through it all and moved to quieter corners – the huge bulk of Roguey drawing me ever closer.

In the distance I could see Billie Maguire standing on a wall and looking all around. I knew that she was wondering where I'd got to and I giggled like a child as she squinted into the sunshine under the shade of her hand. There in her white dress and her flat shoes and all bossy boots as usual.

Things to be done, Billie Maguire, I whispered, things to be done.

As I stepped up on to Roguey Rock for the first time in many years I could feel nothing of the death

I had caused in this place. There was no ghostly fossil collector waiting for his revenge. There were no shivers and no whirling visions of the tumbling man and the silent splash. Only the millions of dead things in the limestone for whom the years, by now, meant nothing.

In a sheltered spot overlooking the deep boiling water, I curled up happily and pulled the hood of the anorak tight around my face. From here I could see everything. Over there, the sunbathers and the screaming children; over there, Billie Maguire watching everything like a hawk and over there, the place where I had murdered a palaeontologist at the age of nine. Far below me the waves swelled hypnotically and I thought about jellyfish and sharks and wondered about the sound of the sea in my ears, and my lungs bursting into darkness.

I must have been up there for hours just thinking about things, talking to the grandmother and showing her the fossils. I was plotting and planning how to steal a JCB so that I might dig up the whole beach by moonlight and uncover the white bones of that great whale I had painted a thousand times and touch those overwhelming bones. How to find the buried Child of Prague that I might bring it home once more – a present for the devoted grandmother – and how to put an end to many things that needed ending here in this sandy cemetery of statues, bones and hubcabs.

And suddenly I heard the voice of Billie Maguire calling my name. And there she was, frantic and breathless, as she hurried along the rocks beneath me, gulls scattering noisily before her – the face scarlet and the coat flapping angrily around her.

Billie! I shouted, Billie! Up here!

Sweet Jesus! she screamed, where the hell were you? You had me going up the walls! My God! I didn't know what had happened to you!

I didn't like her anger and so I made no reply. There was no need for her to be like that with me. No call for that at all. I wasn't doing any harm just sitting up there out of the way and minding my own business.

Come down here! she shouted up at me, we're going now!

As I looked down at Billie Maguire I knew that at last we were about to take our tender walk together. We would step out along the sand and gaze together at the roaring rollers, the showers of diving birds and the red summer sun beginning to set out over America. There would, at last, be just the two of us and I climbed gently down towards her, checking once more for that familiar comforting heaviness half lost in the lining of my coat.

She continued to scold as I hopped on to the sand and she made me promise never to go off and leave her like that again. I told her that I never would and I swore on the granny's grave, my hidden hand beginning to twitch.

C'mon, she said, with just a tiny smile of relief, everyone is waiting for you.

My fingers finally formed a fist around a solid relic which had lain within the cotton wool and sweetie

181

papers of that coat for many years. Last used at this very spot many years ago – when I was nine and the palaeontologist wasn't looking – it was the hammer of the heretics, the tool of the trade.

As Billie Maguire turned to walk away, I gazed at the back of her blurring beautiful head. There were that many torturing voices in the roaring Bundoran wind that I couldn't tell them part. Apart, of course, from the clearest voice of all – that of the sainted grandmother – full of snarling venom and telling me, over and over again, that Billie Maguire was never any good.

And then the sudden explosion as I roared at the grandmother at the top of my lungs to go away and leave me alone. And for a moment I thought that the very rocks would split above me and the sand would suck me into its belly for ever as everything, full of vomiting guilt, went dark and deadly quiet. All I could hear was the sound of my own blood pumping in my own ears.

Billie Maguire looked at me with pity in her eyes and held out her hand. She had heard me scream so many times before.

C'mon, she said gently, we have to go now. You'll be able to do some lovely pictures when we get back. That would be nice, wouldn't it?

In the distance, its door already open, a small white bus.